# CENOTE CITY

## MONIQUE QUINTANA

# CL◀SH

Copyright © 2018 by Monique Quintana

Cover by Joel Amat Güell

ISBN: 978-1-944866-30-3

**CLASH Books**

clashbooks.com

Email: clashmediabooks@gmail.com

*For Juarez—My son, clown, and drumbeat.*

I walk beneath your pens, and am not what I truly am, but what you'd prefer to imagine me.

— JUANA INÉS DE LA CRUZ

# CONTENTS

# *N*UESTROS JUGADORES

**LOPEZ FAMILY**
    Marcina
    Lune
    Nico


**DE LA O FAMILY**
    de la O (Sylvia)
    Jonny Ex Oh
    The Seamer (Ghost Father)


**TINY COVEN**
    Yoli
    Stevie
    Carlo


**THE GENERALES**
    Those that oppress our people

# MAPA

**PARKSIDE**
The Cenote
Storylandia
The Zoo
The Concrete Carnival
The Cemetery

**THE TOWER DISTRICT**
Stevie's Tree House
Yoli's Consignment Shop
Lune and Nico's Apartment

**NORTH SIDE**
The Racetrack
Drive-In Theater
Piper's Pizza

**EAST SIDE**
Santa Muerte Hospital
The Hospital Garden
La Lab
The Fairgrounds

# DEFINICIONES

**CENOTE:** A natural pit, or sinkhole, resulting from the collapse of limestone bedrock that exposes groundwater underneath. Especially associated with the Yucatán Peninsula of Mexico, cenotes were sometimes used by the ancient Maya for sacrificial offerings.

**QUINCEAÑERA:** A celebration of a girl's 15th birthday. It has its cultural roots in Mesoamerica and is widely celebrated today throughout the Americas.

**PAPEL PICADO:** A decorative craft made out of paper cut into beautiful and elaborate designs. It is considered a Mexican folk art. The designs are commonly cut from colored tissue paper.

**CHINAMPAS:** A type of Mesoamerican agriculture which used small, rectangular areas of fertile arable land to grow crops on the shallow lake beds in the Valleys of Mexico.

# $\mathcal{S}$ TORYLANDIA

WHEN LUNE LOPEZ was hired to run Storylandia on her own, she inherited Cora in the last of her days. Lune lived with her mother, Marcrina and her son, Nico in an apartment off of Belmont Avenue. Her mother made her income delivering dead babies and she needed Lune's help to make rent. And even though it was a low paying job, Lune found solace in Storylandia, watching all the people that came and went.

Storylandia is a place where mothers and fathers bring their children to learn about fantastical things right before they tell them to stop believing in fantastical things. It has always been a tiny speck within the bigger O of the park. If you look at a map of Cenote City Park, you would see the zoo and the lake dug deep in the ground with flower buds and wax paper cups floating like fish and you would see the Concrete Carnival dressed in metal and pale painted clown heads and the mouth of a lion, and you would see a roller skating rink and train tracks and you would see Storylandia. For two dollars, you could buy a ticket to Storylandia and stay until the park closed. The park was a hodge podge of nursery rhymes, fairy tales, and Arthurian legends. Jack's beanstalk rose six feet to the sky, a flutter of diamond shaped leaves that could cut your hand if you let them.

Around the time Lune met Cora, a young man

named Alex had begun to come to the park and was trying to get her to fall in love with him. She wondered why because she always wore the same polka-dotted dress to work every day. He told her that he liked her smile and the smell of her rose petal perfume. She told him she got the perfume as a gift from her dead grandmother and yet he still stayed in love with her. She told him she had a teenage son with a razor fade and a mean look. He kept on loving her. He told her that he wanted to meet her son, and she wanted to slap him for having the nerve to say that.

She told the tiny monkey, Cora, all about how she wanted to get rid of the guy and she only laughed, sucking on the pearls around her neck, humming a song in contemplation. She told her that she would make her an anti-love spell with crushed stems from the garden. She had begun to wear a pink dress with matching high heels and white ruffled socks she found in a trunk in the storage shed. On days when Story-landia was slow, she went to live in the cottage of the three bears, its occupants only statues, the paint brown of their fur chipping off of them and fluttering in the wind like insects. Even now, when Lune thinks of the curve of their claws growing in the clouds and the moonlight, she begins to shiver. In the past, no one ever used to stay in Storylandia long enough to see nightfall. Not until Cora began hosting her horror plays.

WHEN LUNE WAS A LITTLE GIRL, all the hospitals in town were doing corrupt things to their patients and everyone knew that what was bad for the humans would be bad for the animals. Doctors and nurses and hospitals administrators began to pour into Storylandia at night to see the plays about the hospitals and the wrongs that were happening in them.

To make extra money for the Storylandia workers, Cora sold tickets cheap at the door, and she hosted the show when the park went quiet and there was only the soft call of birds from the zoo on the other side. Lune imagined them to be bright blue birds calling out, their throats making tiny sutures in the sky. Cora wore a lab coat splattered with red paint, the coat trailing at her legs like a gown. In her voice was the cool rasp of memory, the song of that old zoo mist inside her. The mist that sprayed cool from the pipes lulled her and the other monkeys to sleep in their cage. Sometimes she clasped her throat when she announced it was show time, her paws decked with plastic emeralds and rubies, gifts from the children that came to see her. The same children that took to drawing her face on bathroom walls and playground tunnels in pink chalk. Pink was her favorite color. She was touted as the monkey queen who could bring down the hospitals that were making poor people sicker and sicker, so sick they'd die.

After 3,000 moons, the animals began to call for Cora. They wanted their queen back. They began to haunt the wrappers in the cigars she smoked every morning, and she began to eat less and less every day. Lune began to stay overnight in Storylandia to be with her. They slept in rollaway cots in the wide mouth of the Three Little Pigs House, which was near a tiny forest of trees, their branches scraping and tapping on the fake brick roof. She began to talk in her sleep, the loose letters of her words floating on the warm wind through the tiny houses and pirate ships and castles and ceramic mushrooms that dotted the ground of Storylandia like bones on a beach. Even the fish that lived in the zoo's aquarium began to call for Cora to come back to them, blowing millions of bubbles until their tanks began to explode, the fish lying on their sides, calling out for her, their gills and fins slapping so loudly that she could hear them like drum beats in her ear. Those fish martyred themselves on their smooth side bellies, their slick tails curling up to the moon. They made morning constellations for the zoo-keepers, who swept them up and carried them to their graves in cheap plastic dustpan funerals, Cora's name still swimming through their soft and shattered bones.

The ghosts of old Storylandia park workers appeared to her and begged her to stay with them. They told her there could only be joy for the dead and the living if she would stay. The children that came to see her horror plays had learned to walk with their heads held high, wearing crowns made from dande-lions that Cora herself had helped them cut with pocket knives from the garden.

The last time Lune saw Cora, the Monkey Queen, she was climbing up the beanstalk that grew high in Storylandia. She scaled the wall and flew away from the park. She would not tell her where she was going, and she would not tell her if she would ever return. On the other side of the wall was the old highway with cars like ribbons and motels with neon swimming pools breathing with dust and sweat and long legged dark-skinned beauty queens drawing black chalk sigils in driveways for love and protection.

# BLESSINGS IN JAGUAR EYE

I KNEW the cenote wouldn't be the same after the divers came and kept my mother from her nighttime ritual. You see, my mother cries massive tears every night for hours on end and her body belongs to this city. A long time ago, this city used to be called Flute City, but my mother made the cenote important. Now this is Cenote City and people come to watch my mother cry. Her body isn't entirely her own, it hasn't been for some time now. But tonight, my friends and I will help her escape, so we can take her to a woman that can cure her of her ailments. It's been three weeks since the divers have been here and the cenote water has begun to rise and spill over.

My family needs to leave. Over the years, my mother's house has become a tourist spot or rather, my mother, Marcrina Lopez, has become a tourist spot. Every night she comes out of her house and sits at the wide mouth of the cenote and cries into the water at the bottom. Tonight the sky is so dark that you can't see the colors the way they are really meant to be, but The Generales came to see us today and put up papel picado laced with blinking Christmas lights and those lights will polka dot the place until the sun decides to comes up in all its true and fast fades of pink. I try to come every night to be here with my mother. Some nights I get caught up in other things, but tonight, I'm here.

9

The crying jags came after all the hospitals were forced to close and my mother had turned fifty and her body had begun to turn into something like stone. When I say stone, I mean it in the most beautiful way I can think of. Her shoulder bones became sharp and her waist curved in like an upside down triangle and her hips had the curve of the new moon. Her body became the moon tipping over and over on itself. My mother's voice had become tinged with a rasp and when she laughed in the morning she sounded like a bird with specks of dirt caught in its throat, but still singing and making sounds anyway. She had been delivering dead babies for years when the crying jags came. And she was almost sad when she had to stop delivering the babies, when The Generales forced her to live at the cenote.

She was the first beauty I had ever known in life. My mother had been dying her hair with peroxide and the tone set off her brown skin and slanted eyes to something that was unexpected but fitting. She used to tell people she dyed it to look like Greta Garbo. If you look at Marcrina Lopez from far away, from the dim mist of the cenote, she looks like a girl that I used to see in her green tinged pictures, her golden hair pinned back with honeysuckle flowers, but if you walked up close to her you would see that she was a woman, a woman that believed in such things as demonology and that her body could be riddled with vines and thorns, but she would still be there intact, waiting in the smoke that rises like jaguar eyes.

My mother says I have jaguar eyes, carved into my face, like the eyes of my father. Everyone said that I looked more like my father than my mother. I believe my father still lives on the other side of the valley, past the mountains and vineyards that surround this city. My father has only come to see my mother and I three times since he left when I was a little girl, right before all the hospitals were shut down. My father's face has become something like unmolded clay, like the pots the visitors throw in the hole to make a mockery of our ancestors.

TONIGHT, as the water tips over and over and over itself, I watch my son Nico pick up one of the candles that had been buried under the knotted root of a tree and take it to his grandmother, Marcrina. He has always been the only one who will walk right up to her and she'll speak to him, although her crying always drowns out the sound of their voices, so no one can hear what they're saying to each other. A moment ago there was a blue florescent light coming from someone in the crowd, and that blue light broke up the camera flash of people taking selfies in front of the cenote. I still wonder why The Generales haven't built a barricade to keep people from falling into the hole of water, but then that would keep tourists from throwing things in the cenote, and maybe that's what The Generales want. Maybe they want the tourists to lose themselves in a gape.

All these people throw things in the hole as prayers and watch their relics fade into the water like smoke. This is what keeps all the tourists coming into this city every night. They come to see my mother cry and then they leave. Or sometimes they go to the ruins of the hospital garden and then leave. They always leave eventually. And tonight the cenote is not its old self, the water is filled up to the brim and spilling over in tiny rivers. They have become the same color of the wands of sage that hang from my mother's kitchen window like rabbits. Right now, as I wrap ribbons around my hands in contemplation, I try to imagine how warm the water is below. I imagine myself swimming at the bottom of the cenote, that I have gills that'll make me invincible underwater. The ribbons make a red mark on my hands and I like the way they burn into my skin.

One of the guards whistles at me and taps his fingers on the kitchen window. It's Alex, who used to be my lover, and even though he doesn't have access to my body any more, I let him call me *pink* tonight because that's the color I'm wearing. I'm wearing a bright pink rain slicker for my cenote outfit because the morning weather forecast predicted rain, but all that has come is a faint trickling which seems to make the tourists more delighted and gives them food for their flowers. There are little boys making cups with their hands and collecting the water in them and sprinkling them into the dirt. I wonder why children know more about ritual than we do. The little boys remind me of Nico when he was young and when he used to smile at me more often.

I walk outside into the mist and I hold my slicker away so it doesn't stick to my knees. I've been looking for a mark in the trees or in the sky, but I can only find it in this cheap plastic that I hold and it feels warm between my fingers like a carnival flower. Flower is the word that hangs low in my throat right now. I come across a single purple flower stitched in a checker board patterned pot, and the petals of the flower have cursive writing on them that say, *blessings*. I think about the hands that wrote this word again and again on each petal. I wonder if they mean to say a different blessing for each petal, like it's dead baby skin, or if they mean to write the same exact blessing on each petal, a multitude for my mother to stop crying and be out of her pain. No, I think. They all want to keep coming back here, they want to be here, they want to see her there, they want to see my son here, they want to see me here.

To them, we are famous like stars on old turn dial sets, coated with dust from walls that lean to the east when you walk through them. Those aren't blessings for my family. That's just wishful thinking on my part, and right now, my son's eyes hook in mine from the other side of the cenote. My son's body glows red like a stick of copal there. He can never decide what kind of element he wants to become. I tell him that indecisiveness is the mark of a boy.

I had my son when I was fifteen. My mother never got to meet his father. He was dead before that could happen, and for that, my mother was angry with me. She was angry because she would never have the satisfaction of looking Nico's father in the eye, she would never know just how much Nico did or didn't look like me or his father, she would never really know as much about her grandson as she wanted to know, and for that, she was angry with me and just when it seemed like my mother was ready to forgive me, the crying jags came and that old conversation was lost between us.

My mother used to deliver babies that died in the womb. The mobile clinics would only pass into the city once a month, and so Marcrina fulfilled a necessity, something to help quell the sting of the pain. Womb pain. The first baby she delivered was the child of a butcher's wife. She had never been to their side of town before and needed to call a cab to take her there. You have to call a cab at least eight hours ahead of time here because hardly no one uses them, but when she arrived at the butcher's house, she was welcomed and fed dinner and even given a small clean room to sleep in after the baby was born. She scrubbed her hands with blue soap and tangerine rinds and said a spell for the woman's blood and for the child's blood as well. The child came out so intact, so unblemished in its form, that she took it's pulse to make sure it wasn't just sleeping. And with the birthing of that child, she felt a certain peace then. She began to realize that that was what she was meant to do. She tapped the baby gently on the throat and then tapped lower and felt the bone beneath. She took to doing that for every baby birth thereafter. There was a song written there by each child, the expanse of the negative, shimmering seeds in their marrow, a garden of blessings.

 A LUNE

MY SON HAS magic in all of his blood. My mother will never know this, but Nico looks a lot like his father's family. Nico was born during the full moon with free earlobes and a full head of curly jet-black hair and eyes the color of sap. He was born at the foot of my bed on striped sheets and a plastic pink shower curtain, escaping from my bones to his grandmother's hands. If his father had been there, he would have watched his son come out, unafraid of the sight of blood and he would have tattooed his son's name on the web of his hands, but he wasn't there, alive and in his body. I could only imagine his ghost sitting between the red and black candle flame that my mother set on the windowsill to celebrate her grandson's new skin. She had made the candles herself. There was a red candle for power and a black candle for protection. My mother bathed Nico quickly with a yellow sponge from the sea and cradled him between her palms and hummed a song that was unrecognizable to me.

People always ask me what it's like to have a baby without the drugs and I always refuse to tell them. Maybe it's because I wanted to know what those injections would feel like, the medicine running sick and happy through my veins. Maybe it was because I was jealous of them because they had the money to go

15

to a hospital on the other side. I hear stories about the babies born on the other side of the valley. All those babies are delivered by pale-faced men with eyes like azure and hair like gold.

Nico was the only living baby that my mother ever delivered. When a baby had died before it could leave the tomb of its mother, women would call my mother to deliver the baby. My mother charged them half the price as the doctor and she always took care of the burial if they wanted her to. She did a ritual for the baby so that it will journey safely to the other side. *The other side of what?* I always asked her and she never replied, only handed me the flower pot that we would leave on the gravestone, if the family had the money to even buy a stone.

My mother's work delivering babies ended when her crying jags began. Nico and I were living with her in her apartment on Belmont when they began. Our kitchen window had the view of a funeral home, and I was watching a procession of low rider cars move slowly down the street like ants from a hill when I heard my mother crying uncontrollably. I always thought it was strange how much crying sounded like laughing. She was crying and hiccupping as she put on her liquid eyeliner in the medicine cabinet mirror. My tiny mother, shaking in her tight red dress and patent leather stiletto shoes. Her face was streaked with black mascara starbursts and the purple red tinge of her eye shadow. My mother in her mask.

Marcrina Lopez cries a lot.

*This isn't the first time this has happened to me,* she said. *It hurts like hell.*

16

# DRAPES

A FEW WEEKS AGO, Alex, the guard was staring at me through the window of Yoli's consignment shop. I could see his face through the handbags that were hung up in the window like half moons, red and brown and yellow half moons of dull and shimmery textiles that were working in my favor to block out both the sun and Alex's face. It was hot that day and there were tiny electric fans in all the nooks and crevices of the store. They sat on top of shelves, on the counter next to the cash register, and on the floor, the little wind of them cooling my ankles as I walked by them.

I walked through the racks and racks of clothes. I looked for colors. Every time I walked close to the window, Alex seemed to shake a little from the other side of the glass and that made me laugh out loud. I looped through the racks the way serpents looped through trees. I imagined that my body was a cylindrical thing, a skin covered with scales that would illuminate like stones if I made it back outside, if someone set me to the sidewalk and into the sunlight. When I heard Yoli's shoes click clack their way back to the cash register, I stopped the looping and set myself on a rack full of vintage suits. I pulled out a pant suit and tried to smell the old in it, the body that used to be in there, but I couldn't. I thought that this was a sign that the body was dead. Yoli always laundered

17

and steamed the clothes that she thought she could make a little more money from, and instead of smelling decay, the suits smelled to me like a garden spilled out, like daffodils and daises with rainclouds clotted fresh with dirt.

"There are some new things in there!" Yoli called out to me.

I pulled out a metal heart shaped hanger with a white jacket and matching pants tucked inside it. In the lining of the jacket, there were initials that I couldn't make out because the thread was coming undone. Yoli walked over me, holding a white fedora with a cherry red band. The band looked like little drops of blood on dirty snow. She put the hat on my head and smiled at me. I wanted to stick my finger in the tiny dimple that peeked out of her smile. Her big green eyes scanned my face and then settled on my hips.

"This'll be a good fit. This goes with that," she said.

She made an imaginary arrow from the hat on my head and the suit that was hooked to my hand. I glanced at the window to see if Alex was still there, but he wasn't. A group of girls walked by the window laughing behind their hands. One had her dark hair pulled back in a ponytail, a fake rabbit tail looped on the top. I wondered why she felt like she was unlucky. I thumbed at the stone and the quarters in my pocket and wished that Alex were still there in the window.

"I'm pretty sure that's a guy's suit, but it must have been a tiny guy. I couldn't pass this up. If no one buys it, I'm keeping it for myself."

"I want to try it on. Do you think it'll fit me?"

Yoli laughed and walked back to the register, pulling her cat eye glasses over her face.

"You look very clever with those glasses on, Yuri!"

"Yeah, yeah, what the fuck ever," she laughed. I could tell that she wanted the zoot suit for herself.

I waved the suit in the air, and she nodded at me without even looking up. She had begun to pull slips out from drawers behind the counter and she was marking them with a fat black crayon in a furious way.

I made my way towards the back of the store to the dressing rooms. The dressing rooms are cubbyholes in the wall with oval mirrors that Yoli has decorated with black lace and green glow-in-the-dark puff paint. I walked into the cubby and shut the large gold curtain behind me, so that I was entombed, save for the warm glow of two light bulbs that sprayed my skin in yellow and white. They were screwed in haphazardly on the wall above me and looked like two eyeballs on a face that was missing a mouth and a nose and ears. There were only these two eyes watching my skin, watching my dress fall to the floor like copal in a heap and watching the drapes fold over my body. The jacket hung over my shoulders like it thought it could tell me a secret. My breasts hung tight below the lapel like they could talk back to whatever the jacket said. I worried my perfume would make the jacket smell like me before I even knew if I wanted to buy it. The pants were high waisted, so I couldn't see my belly button, but I could see the half moon scar that marked the end pass of my rib cage. I put my finger to my scar and felt the bone beneath it.

I felt the cold metal almost cut my face, before I even felt the curtain fall open and then close again around me. I waited for applause, I waited for the shedding on my skin, the new and white textile falling from the dark of my flesh.

Alex held a short blade to my face. The lights flickered on and off. I wanted to resist Alex because he worked for The Generales, but I liked how it smelled like his leather jacket was burning in that moment. I ran my hand gently over the blade, pulled it from his hand and held it to his face. I pulled his left jacket sleeve all the way up to his elbow with my nails. My nails shimmered red in the glow of that closet and his breathing was growing in syncopation with the rustling of voices outside and the slow beat of the cash register. I pulled the white brim of the hat over my face and put my mouth to his and laughed when I saw that his eyes were closed. I pushed him onto the pink velvet seat and straddled him. I put him inside me and thrust until I came, the blade handle in my hand. He kissed my neck and I put the blade to his face again. *You'll pray to me like I'm a fucking altar next time. You see this blade. You try to touch me without asking and you'll be hanging off this real fast.* I let him hear the beat of my high heels as I walked to the register, the zoot suit over my shoulder like a sigil. I could feel him behind me as I pulled a fat wad of dirty bills from my wallet to pay. He tapped me gently on my shoulder and I could smell his sweat and feel the breeze that rustled through the shop window, *The Generales know*, he said to me softly. *They know that you want to take your mother away. You best leave here at the right time.*

# NIGHT DIVE INTO DEATH COLONIES

THAT NIGHT THE DIVERS CAME, they upset the water of our ancestors. They rapped softly on the door of my mother's house as if they knew about manners and respect, but we knew much better than that. I had sent Nico to pick up some food and I thought the knocking was him coming back. I yelled at him for not using his key. I peeked out the window and saw the guards shaking like flowers, not like they were cold or had lost their life, but because they had just been freshly watered. The divers wore yellow suits and black masks over their eyes and their mouths and they hovered over the cenote as the night sky turned six different shades. They had brought a crew with them and a small boat and when they lowered the boat down into the water with rope, I could hear my mother pulling her own hair, the song of her scalp mingled with the song of the birds who nipped at the rope and I wondered why The Generales would send them here and what they were trying to accomplish.

When Nico got there and saw that the divers were there, he locked himself in my mother's room and refused to come out, even when I begged him to. It would be a busy night. The tourists were lined up down the street and were beginning to spill into the cemetery down the road, and I could hear one of the guards running around yelling for the cash box. Lucy the dog went to the mouth of the cenote and began to

21

bark down at it, the way she did at people when my mother took her out for morning walks. My mother ran for Lucy and cradled her. I heard a window slide open and Nico yell that the divers looked something like bumble bees and my mother said that they were worse, that they were mucosos, despite the brilliant color of their suits.

"Do those divers want to die?" I asked Alex who sat at my mother's front door.

He looked at me and smiled, the scent of his sweat mixed with soap and cigarette smoke. He tapped my shoulder.

"They know that they don't have much time."

The other guards began to let people in, taking the admission fee and putting the money in their white leather vests. Two blonde women standing at the front of the line looked me up and down and laughed.

"What the fuck are you laughing at?" I asked them. A cool breeze grazed my neck. The guard looked at me, smoothed his hair and smiled.

"Don't get all upset for nothing, doll."

"Don't call me that."

"You live in a doll's house."

"I don't live here. This is my mother's house. She's the only one that really lives here. You all know that."

The tourists began to make their way towards the cenote just as the divers began to emerge from the water. They looked into that hole in the earth and began to jump and shout and point at the tiny boat that was bobbing yellow in the water.

*Why can't we go down there?* I heard some of them saying. I could see my mother sitting on her favorite tree root, wearing a purple smock and her favorite pair of black leather cowboy boots. Her hair tossed in the wind like kelp, and I saw that she too was staring at the boat. I began to run over to her, but then I felt Nico tug at my arm and pull me into the house. We watched from the kitchen as the divers' crew began to pull the boat out of the cenote with rope and wire.

"Puppets. They're all fuckin' puppets," Nico said.

"Don't say that. You used to like puppets when you were a baby. Do you remember when my mom bought you that puppet at Olivera Street?"

"What happened to that puppet?" He asked me.

"I haven't seen it in years," I replied.

I was lying to him about that puppet. I had tossed the puppet away years ago because it had lost one of its limbs and its strings had become tangled. My mother had yelled at me for doing this because she had bought it for Nico one of the few times he had travelled out of the valley, and I thought that maybe she had loved that puppet even more than Nico did.

The tourists began to clap and cheer as the divers neared the surface of the water. The tallest diver pulled a sack from the boat and clung to it tightly. The divers were breathing heavily and shooed the pressing tourists away with their rubber arms. A young male reporter from the local news ran up to the divers and his camera crew surrounded them like a slow halo of skin and hair and bone.

"What did you find, sir? What's in the bag?"

There were no answers from the divers.

Nico ran up to the man and began to tug at the bag.

"You can't take that! You shouldn't have even gone down there!"

I yelled out Nico's name and felt it echo in the clamor of voices. I ran out of the house and was hit with the smell of the dirt and the sweat of skin, not of my own blood or people. All this came from these people that didn't belong to us. Energy that didn't belong to us.

The diver slapped Nico across the face and threw him to the ground. I lunged for him and began to claw at his face. All I could smell was the cruel sweat of the diver and then a flashlight tapped softly at my neck. I felt Alex whisper on my throat.

"Fuck that guy, doll. Look, your mother's about to cry."

# PEARLS IN COFFINS

EVERYONE IN TOWN began to speculate about what was in the bag that the divers took from the cenote but all I wanted to know was what they had seen when they got to the bottom. Some of the tourists said the diver that was carrying the bag looked like he was limping, as if the contents of the bag were heavy, but Nico had touched the bag and said that it felt more delicate than it looked, that he thought it felt something like soft wood, like the trees that surround the cenote after it rains.

My mother thought that they carried heads inside the bags and that it was a shame that they had removed them from their proper place for eternity. She said that stealing these skulls was the equivalent of men diving for oysters and slicing out the meat or removing the pearls. They all belonged in the water and removing them from their coffin was a curse to the men who committed such thievery. She said that it was thievery of the worst kind. Nico told her that maybe it was a good thing that the divers took the heads then because they deserved to be cursed for diving in the water in the first place.

After all the pearl talk, I told Nico I felt angry at my mother for making me think of the beach. I told him while we washed the breakfast dishes in our apartment. He was washing, and I was rinsing in luke-warm water. I asked him to be careful. They were my favorite blue plates and cups. My mother had bought them for me at a beachside store when Nico was a baby. I hadn't been to the beach in so long, and I could hardly remember what it looked like. He thought this was strange because he could remember exactly what the beach was like. He reminded me that he had come along with us on our last beach trip. He was small, but he could still remember how cold the water was and how he had tiny insect bites on his feet from walking on the beach barefoot at night.

*That was it*, I told him. That's why I thought I couldn't remember the way the beach looked. It was because we had gone at night. It was pitch dark and we decided to walk along the part of beach that was closed to visitors. Lucy was a pup back then and we brought her with us, her feet dancing and she barked at the waves as they rushed in like giant gnashing teeth. Nico recalled how the beach looked like Mars because there were no humans in sight, only the dark void that I knew was a lie. There were things in those black waters that we couldn't see.

*What do you think was inside that water?* Nico asked me. I told him that I thought there were jellyfish and mermaids with blue hair and scales on their faces that gave them life enough to come to the surface when the sky was awash in sunlight, and that there were birds that had died of exhaustion and had buried their own bones in the cold layers of sea sand, reciting their rites until their vocal chords drowned and were gone. I told him that I thought that beach might be a good place to lay my own body down to sleep and then to die, that the smell of white sage would burn new and clean and be different there. That I would be happy to close my eyes there, that I gave him permission to close my eyelids, if the halting of my breathing hadn't already done the job. He could close my eyes with his fingers and sew them shut because I was his mother and he was my son.

He looked at me and said, *no mother. I was talking about the cenote. I wonder what's at the bottom of the cenote.*

# S TEVEN SANCHEZ
## (THE CLOWN OF EVERYTHING)

I WANTED to tell my friends about my plan to steal away my mother. I had even practiced the way I would tell them, talking to myself in hot showers so that I could hear my voice echo and the plans would make more sense to me. I wanted to tell them the day of the racetrack quinceañera just a few weeks ago, the promise of seeing them made my throat nervous, there was a delight in the terror of it. My friends are my three corners, my tiny coven. I wanted to find Stevie before he left to catch the bus to the quinceañera. Stevie was studying to be The Clown of Everything but to make money he worked weekdays at a pizza restaurant on the corner of Shields and First. This pizza restaurant has a one hundred year old organ that plays a song every fifteen minutes. There's no one there at the organ playing it. It plays itself. When I was a kid, I tried to find out how this was possible, but I got no answer and was satisfied with that.

The restaurant was packed with brown children having birthday parties and even though the restaurant was dim-dark and empty of my friend, I kept looking anyway, the shrill of the organ's song like a dull ache in my ears. It was playing a rabbit song that my mother used to sing to me when I was a little girl. I had forgotten the words for years, but in that moment the words to the song bumped in my head like a bag of stones, and I imagined them to be the same pink and yellow hues of the cone hats of the children. I found the owner's daughter, Kamidee tinkering with an ailing carousel horse that was speckled with stars and half moons.

"Stevie didn't come to work today, he called in sick. Sucks for me," said Kamidee.

I found myself chipping away at the peeling paint of the horse's companion and Kamidee laughed like a bell.

"If Nico's looking for work, I can put him to it. He can clean the organ pipes if you don't want him to be at the counter. I'm always the best at dealing with the assholes anyway."

"I'll let him know. I think a job would be good for him. But I'd only want him to work on the weekends. I don't want a job to distract him from his school work, but I know you wouldn't work him too hard."

"No, and besides. I've got the feeling that Stevie will be quitting soon. Or my mom will fire him. One or the other," Kamidee said. She bumped her hip against the horse and the carousel began to move again.

I wondered if Stevie was really sick, or if he had forgotten to request the time off from work to sing at his cousin's quince. I had left Nico at home by himself, but he had a cell phone, a dog, a gun, candles, and baseball bat and that was a checklist he himself was proud of and took refuge in. I ordered a small pizza for takeout and was waiting by the fortune teller machine when I saw a young man at the pay phone booth. The young man had slick black hair and glasses and smiled at me nervously. The pay phone booth was dotted with lights and pictures of black Vampiras and black Bride of Frankensteins that had been ripped out of a coloring book and pasted to the booth as if it was a papier maché project.

Kamidee must have noticed I was staring at the booth because she said, "I draw my own things. I love the adult coloring books they have now."

"Adult? That sounds funny."

"What's funny about it? I ordered those special from a bookseller in France. Over there adult just means grown up."

A little boy walked up to me and put his arms around my waist and they felt sticky on my blouse. The boy must have mistook me for his mother because when he peered up my face he looked frightened and ran away. The young man in the booth was still watching me and smiling and this made me shiver. The organ began to play a new song and the lights in the place grew dimmer. The birthday kids ran up to the organ and began to pump their fists. Some were holding tiny piñatas dangling from sticks. I ran my hands along the wooden rail that led me out of that place, feeling all the things etched there, three word love notes, phone numbers, curses, and before I reached the door, there was a circle that was dotted with what looked like a tiny tree and a river. I looked back and saw the dark haired man sitting in the corner of the restaurant. He had a pitcher of beer and a large stack of papers sitting on the table in front of him. The young man had slanted eyes that were cat-like in the dark. He waved goodbye to me and mouthed something through the pounding of the organ.

WHEN I GOT to Stevie's place, I could feel the moon begin to turn over and over on itself. Stevie lives in a tree house in the back of a dilapidated mansion that is owned by a white couple that sells their embryos to people who have left Cenote City for happier places. Stevie never opens the door until I call him on the phone and I tell him that I'm outside. This is a game we play as friends. He doesn't want to open the door to unnecessary transactions, he says. Stevie has a stocky build and his beard always seemed to lean towards the east.

He poured me some Earl Grey tea in a chipped cup that said Santa Cruz and had a picture of a pink conch shell on it. The grooves of the conch shell puffed out and I thought it was a nice detail and felt a little jealous that Stevie might have gone to the beach without inviting me. I had never seen the cup before. He must have noticed that I had taken a liking to the cup and told me it was a gift from his clown teacher, Professor Mundo, who he had had a crush on for the last three semesters of school.

"Wow, what's he doing bringing you a souvenir cup?"

"He brought one for everyone who's working on his exhibition. I think he went there with his mom or something. His mom likes to take glass blowing workshops in Capitola and they go to downtown Santa

Cruz to buy books and shit. I think it's nice he does things with his mom."

"Fuck Capitola. But I do want to go to the beach though."

"Meeee too! That's what I'm saying," Stevie laughed as he threw himself on his brass bed, the whole thing letting out a squeal that sounded like a violin on crack. I remembered that my mother had made the bedspread for him years ago, and now the pattern's fading off and is patchy. It has a bunch of robots with bobbed black hair, red lipstick and green high heels, their mouths spouting jajajajajajajajajaja-jajajaja into plastic talking bubbles, the kind you see in comic books or on your cell phone when you're texting someone back and forth. He was playing with his hair and staring at the ceiling sky.

"We should see if the lord and lady would let you cut a little window up there. That would be sweet. You could see the birds and moon and all that."

"I wouldn't even know how to do that," Stevie replied.

"We could figure it out. Maybe Nico could do it. He'll do it if I pay him," I said quietly, but then I noticed that Stevie wasn't listening to me. His eyes were closed as if he were sleeping, but I knew he wasn't. I sat on his old blue armchair, not noticing that his mariachi suit was already sitting there. The brass buttons felt cold and stabbed my thighs. I took the jacket and pants and rocked them in my arms like it was a dead baby, then draped them over my lap and began to write to an imaginary lover in the black velvet.

"When will you leave, Stevie?"

He gets the shivers right before he has to sing and that's why I had gone looking for him in the first place. For me, everything is about looking for the patterns in my friends. Stevie always gets nervous when he has to sing and I could feel it as soon as the sun had crept into my bedroom window that morning. I remembered the tea that Stevie had made for me, but found that it had already turned cold and the tea bag was floating at the bottom.

"What's your solo today?"

"La Llorona."

"Oh, that one! An oldie but goodie."

"All mariachi songs are fucking old," he laughed. "Will you come with me to the party?"

"Yeah! I haven't been to a quinceañera in years."

"The theme is under the sea."

"That's always the theme."

"I'm sort of embarrassed to ask, but how much did these digs cost? All these hand-stitched flowers drip money."

"I don't know. Ben bought them."

Ben was Stevie's brother-in-law, his sister's husband and he was the grand Jefe of the mariachi group, the last mariachi group in the city. To be The Clown of Everything, Stevie had to learn how to be a proper mariachi. This group painted their faces like they were dead because that had been a tradition that was handed from one generation of mariachis to the next. They weren't day of the dead kind of dead. That kind of dead was far too sacred to play year round. They were more like vampire dead, holding a lamp to their faces, so that they could trace out their veins with blue eyeliner that they sharpened to such a point that it sometimes made their face bleed, but that only added to the appeal of it. Sometimes Stevie would draw a thick, veiny heart with butterflies sucking out its chambers. He was left handed, so the pictures he painted always came out a little blurry and so the four other members of the group could never duplicate it.

Stevie went behind his black and green striped screen to get dressed, and I put more water to boil on the stove. The stove was dotted with skull stickers from the pizzeria and stethoscope magnets from the mobile clinic. I began to giggle when I thought about the time that me and Stevie and Nico had chased the trailer down for two blocks because they needed a flu shot, and Stevie was too broke to buy condoms. Nico howled because he knew that was the only way to get the trailer to stop because he was a child, not a small child, but still a child.

The quinceañera was at the racecar track. I found a seat alone in the bleachers because I didn't think I'd know anyone at the party. All the kids were dancing on a platform in the center of the track. Stevie hid underneath the bleachers with his band mates until they got their cue to come out. The birthday girl wore a blue off-the-shoulder dress with a hem that looked like a tulip and she had an eyeball patch stitched to her hip. *Protection, a good thing*, I thought, *Evil eyes are everywhere at a quince*. Just as I was thinking about evil eyes, I felt someone rub on my leg from underneath the bleachers. Through the slit I could see that it was

Ben. He was short, with blondish hair and blue eyes like a Spaniard.

"Don't you dare touch me! You're a married man!" I shouted at him. I got up and went to sit on the other side of the bleachers, but I could still hear the voices of the mariachis humming below like insects, and I began to tap my feet on the bleachers, thankful for a cool breeze that felt like it had sliced my neck in two. All the teens were doing a synchronized dance, the thumping from the speakers coming out loud like a drum.

There was a giant cake the shape of coral reef on the platform, which seemed a little out of place but it looked like it tasted good and I hoped that I could eat some. I only ate cake a few times a year. There aren't a lot of reasons to eat cake in this city. Off in the distance, the drive-in movie theater had just begun to play *A Place in the Sun* and Montgomery Cliff's large dark eyes were better than the streetlights.

MY PHONE BEGAN to buzz with a text message from Nico asking when I'd get home. He wanted to go to the cenote before midnight and he wanted me to come with him. I replied that I would be home as soon as I could. The sky began to fade to a different shade of pink, like the insides of a seashell, and the trumpet blare of the mariachis put a knock in my bones. I stood up so I could see better, holding my skirt closed around me, but then I let it go, so that it blew in the hot wind like a dandelion.

The dead mariachis crept out from under the bleachers with grace in the fading light, the dust from the racecars like clouds of smoke. They emerged, black-cloaked and shimmering. The five mariachis walked out in a single file line and stopped in between the cake and Elizabeth Taylor's face looming in the background. They dropped their long black capes to the floor.

Stevie stepped out from the five, pulling a long stemmed blooming flower from his throat, and he began to sing, writing the shape of each word in the air before him, the tenor of his voice like a scissor slit to the sky, and for the first time, I wondered if anyone could tell that he really didn't speak Spanish, that as soon as he stopped singing the enunciation would retract back into the throat like old black video tape. He had drawn an orange butterfly on his cheek, its wings stitched to its body with thread. I felt like I was friends with Stevie's butterfly because I had watched him draw it at the tree house and the kids dancing on the racetrack didn't know about all the intricate parts of it like I did and this made me feel honored.

All the kids had their phones out, and they were recording the mariachi band, the phones were aimed right at Stevie because he was the star, a brown crush against the black velvet and brass. His violin on his hip, their mouths open wide like an O. The cars ran the track like hot zippers in concrete, little spirals of wire growing out of the cars like vines. Stevie sang on and on amongst the whir of cars, Elizabeth Taylor's eyes wide in the background, the sky growing darker and darker,

Montgomery Cliff's crooked longing and a flurry of ballerina tulles and thrift store bridal gowns. I stood on top of the bleachers and clapped my hands as loud as I could, even though I knew that my rhythm was always off. I wanted Stevie to hear me and it seemed liked he did because he looked up at me and waved with a quiet ferocity that I had never seen on him before.

When the music stopped, I hopped off the bleachers and ran across the racetrack as fast as I could, all the quinceañera kids running too, flapping against me like wings. The girls screamed, clutching their high heels in their hands. The few girls that were in the quinceañera party held up their matching dresses like they were great doñas exposing glow bracelets and rub-on tattoos of roses and unicorns and pentagrams. They surrounded the mariachi band and asked to take pictures with them. Stevie had the most kids asking for pictures because he was the lead singer and was the most handsome of the group. There was no orderly line to take a picture with Stevie like there was a line to get into the cenote, and I found it surprisingly refreshing to have to clamor for the opportunity to speak to my own friend. A young man who was wearing a sailor cap nudged me in front of some girls.

"You get in there," he said. He smiled at me and he made me think about Nico. He was wearing pomade that smelled like mango.

"Will you take my picture with this fine gentle-man?" I asked the sailor boy.

Stevie put his arm around me and laughed.

37

"Make sure you take a couple of them. I always blink in pictures," I told the boy.

My camera flashed bright and made me feel dizzy.

"Hey Stevie. We gotta get out of here," Ben yelled. He pulled off Stevie's sombrero and tossed it down the stairs that ran below the platform. It felt like the racecars were running up and down my spine.

There was a collective sigh from all the kids and then a multitude of thank-yous and blessings as I followed the mariachi band down the stairs.

.

# $\mathcal{T}$HE BEAUTIFUL BELOW

MY GIRL, Yoli the dressmaker, was wrapping red tulle around a mannequin and our friend Carlo was painting the mannequin's fingernails black. They were both shaking with laughter, but when they heard us coming down the stairs, they stopped and began to clap their hands.

"Bravo, my babies! You all were great up there," Yoli said, laughing. She popped a pink bubble gum bubble from her brown lip-sticked mouth. She was wearing a silver snake cuff on her elbow and it had purple eyes like Elizabeth Taylor does in real life. Marc touched the snake on its head and it hissed and snapped at him.

I touched the snake too, but the snake just looked at me with its narrow eyes and then retracted back to Yoli's arm, squeezing it until she yelled for her to stop.

"Is that a gift from your aunt?" I asked her. Her aunt is always sending her good gifts from the other side. Her aunt was a doctor my mother worked with years ago, a woman I always heard everyone call by her last name, de la O. Yoli calls her Aunt Sylvia.

"If you like it you can have it," she said, uncoiling the bracelet from her arm and letting it pass to my own. It wrapped around me firmly and quickly and the tiny pinch of it felt really good.

Carlo was fixing the mannequin's hair into a

beehive, a giant red beehive. He stood back to admire his work.

"Watch this," he said.

Bees began to fly out of the mannequin's hair and they looked so beautiful that I forgot to scream.

"I put a spell on that hive. So that you and your son will have a safe trip to the other side."

"How did you know about that, Carlo? How did you know that I'm thinking about leaving?"

Carlo acted like he didn't hear me say that. There were no more words from any of them. And the only thing that flew around us were the bees.

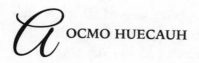

# OCMO HUECAUH

WHEN JONNY DE LA O was still a boy, his mother saw that he was sleeping with his eyes open. She was one of the most respected doctors in the valley, but even she couldn't understand what was ailing him. It was nearing winter, even though fall and winter were of little distinction in the city. The fog began to hang on the windows with the seeming promise of love. Jonny was fourteen and ran in the halls of his high school with all the humor of a boy his age. He had always been a cheerful boy, but sleep had become his strange place and mother de la O couldn't understand why. She did know that he had just finished reading Poe in his Horror Lit class, and at first she thought that he was sleeping with his eyes open as a sort of joke to amuse her, as he often did, but it kept happening night after night and she knew that she would have to come up with some kind of remedy or hope that the thing would pass or become something else more tolerable.

Jonny had done things in his sleep before. He had begun to sleepwalk at the age of three, the year that she had gotten together with Tim, a kind, blonde-haired doctor man she had met that spring when he transferred to her hospital.

The first time she had seen Tim, he was walking through the hospital corridor with a young woman, a patient with brown hair and brown skin the color of a

41

bruised apricot, a red ribbon weaved loose through each braid that grazed her shoulder blades. The woman's gown fell in a moment, and Tim pinched the gown closed with his fist. Dr. de la O found herself walking over to them and offering to see the woman back to her room. She exchanged her own hand for Tim's. He smiled at her gently. She could see that he was younger, not too much younger, but young enough for her to feel a small ache in her stomach. She had noticed young men weren't looking at her any more. The woman shivered below her hand, and when she helped her into her bed, the woman smiled at her weakly, but gripped her hand, the scent of jasmine passing through the woman's wrists and her braids. A week later, the young woman was dead.

Tim told de la O of the woman's passing over dinner. *She was a nice girl*, he had told her. *Too young to be sick and die like that*, he said over the flicker of his lighter to cigarette, the promise of love hanging over the patio of the hospital cafeteria. They were both doctors. Breathing bodies came and went, that was one thing they could be certain of and de la O let her fall into the man because of uncertainty, her hand upon his white coat, shivering, the warm glow of hospital lights, an offering, his pale hand, an offering, clasped on hers, his mouth a slow digital beat, an offering.

She had sex with Tim every night in her house, his pale skin eclipsing her dark skin through the lace opening of her gown. Every night she marveled at his white skin glowing in the moonlight. When it was over, she lay in bed as Tim rolled over and fell asleep.

She could hear the scratching of the oak trees on the window like they were angry with her and she couldn't understand why. There were two things that she always prayed would not disrupt her. Jonny, or a phone call from the hospital. Jonny, whose small steps she'd hear patter across the wooden floors at night.

*This is a happy house, this a happy house* she would recite to herself as if it was a prayer. It was the very thing that the previous owner had told her when she bought the house..

*This is a happy house, this is a happy house,* her own feet picking up tiny speed as she walked through the house to find Jonny. She would find him walking towards the dining room window, a window she kept bare so that they could see the hospital garden in the distance. Jonny would be walking towards the glass, like it was a door and he could open it with an invisible key. She could see the Santa Muerte statue in the hospital garden swinging in the dark, her robe a slash in the large rustling leaves. de la O had learned from a colleague that talking to sleepwalkers could make them violent and agitated, so she took to holding him gently by the shoulders and walking him back to bed.

Now there was no sleepwalking, just his brown open eyes, slanted and unflinching. She began to take to closing his bedroom door, even though it had always made her feel safe to leave it open, so that she could always see him. In the deep blue of the night, she watched Jonny's bedroom door and when she grew tired, she learned to listen for his opening door, the smile and sigh of hinges to let her know she was needed.

43

She began to feel as if she was being consumed from the waist down. At night, Tim began to climb on top of her with a ferocity that she couldn't understand. The ferocity grew and grew with passing weeks, and his body split hers apart in love or something else. Her groin tickled slick and she held it with her hand when trying to sleep on her stomach or behind a tree when she tried to take a walk in the light autumn rain. Her legs floating below her, wondering, her hand on her groin, the ring on her pinky finger shaking.

It was snowing in the city. It was the first snow that had fallen in decades. de la O asked Jonny to go for a walk in the cemetery to visit his father's grave. He didn't want to go with her and only agreed when she promised that she would buy him lunch at Pyramid Burger. He asked her for a milkshake with a cherry on top. Going to Pyramid Burger had become a secret between her son and herself. Tim was repulsed by the place, not because it was a fast food joint but because it was in Parkside and he hated going to Parkside. The snowfall was light. A specter of snow. And even though it wasn't enough to make any kind of creature, de la O was grateful for it. Even though it was cold, or maybe because it was cold, Jonny insisted that they eat outside. The wind was like a hollow drumbeat on the overhang, and de la O knew that her son thought of the little shelter that surrounded them as a concrete palace.

"What kind of snow is this?" he asked her without

even looking at her. He was wearing a green hooded sweatshirt that he got from being in multi-media club, a thing he had joined because he thought it would get him a girlfriend, even though she told him that he was too young to have one.

The snow fell on the street and disappeared into the gray of it. Tire marks streaked the ground like chalk and the grill smelled like onions and meat and de la O's body began to feel consumed again. The red and gold lights of the place began to start up again, flickering joyfully on the large screen monitor, like it was the marquis to a show they had never seen before.

"Those lights remind me of Las Vegas," de la O told her son.

He smiled at her and he said, "Why do you say that to me? When you've never even taken me there? It makes me sad."

Across the street, she could see a groundskeeper walking around the cemetery with a rake, walking in circles on the grass and bumping into tombstones, as if he were dancing. She had met him once, when she had gone to take flowers to Jonny's father. She had yelled at him because a sprinkler had been left on overnight and had flooded the small red rectangle planter that she had put there in honor of her dead. The man was small and brown like her, with the faintest shadow of a beard. She imagined that he must have been old enough to be her father's age and in turn, she began to apologize over and over again to him, her shame seeping in with the cold itch of the grass on her ankles. She felt her stiletto dig in the dirt, and she cursed herself for yelling at the man when he didn't deserve it. She pulled a yellow flower from the planter and said, *See, these are ugly flowers anyway*. On the other side of the gravel cemetery road, a lone mariachi sang "Volver" out of tune, and she carried the red planter away from the place and never brought it back to her dead man again.

Now, she was sitting on the other side with her son and she felt like her body was being consumed.

"Tim is aocmo huecauh," Jonny said.

"What are you talking about?"

"Aocmo huecauh."

de la O took the first drink of her own milkshake and contemplated the chocolate in her throat.

"You know, our ancestors invented chocolate," she said to her son.

"Yeah, they weren't aocmo huecauh like Tim. Let's go. Don't you have to get ready to go to the hospital?"

"Aren't you going to eat your food?" de la O asked her son.

"I'm not hungry," he said. "Besides it's cold as fuck out here, and I hate eating inside this place. Can we go to see my dad tomorrow instead?"

THE TINY SNOW had stopped by the time de la O got to the hospital. She found that her floor was quiet, expect for the soft murmur of nurses still remarking from the snow and the slow beat of machines. She searched for a voice that she recognized more than the others. She began to listen for Marcrina's voice, even though Marcrina wasn't expected that day. There was a plastic doll lying on top of the counter at the nurse's station. de la O went to the nurse's station and pulled a cotton ball from a jar and dabbed her fingers wet with alcohol wipes. The doll on the counter had blue eyes and thick black lashes that curled up and pale blonde curls tucked into a snood at the nape of her neck. There was a tag wrapped around the wrist of the doll. de la O thumbed the wrist of the doll and wished that the doll could talk and tell her where she came from.

de la O rolled the cotton ball in her fingers and walked on her hospital path. There was usually someone waiting near her office to talk to her, but not on that day. The doors to each hospital room were lit with the blue glow of their television sets, mounted on the wall of each room like a mouth, welcoming her to step into the warm shadows they cast on this floor scrubbed clean with quiet hands. A pink balloon with confetti was caught in the hinge of her office door. She pulled it out and the balloon's ribbon was twisted and frayed like stands of hair. She didn't know if the balloon would float or bounce along the floor but she left it alone in the hallway and locked the door behind her. She dared to leave her curtains opened because the sky was dark, and she knew that there was no one in the garden. She went to her desk and dialed the pharmacy. There was no answer and she wondered why.

She sat on her chair and parted her legs and the cotton ball fell to the floor, quiet like the snow that had come and gone, and she pulled her panties down the purple crush of the lace, only a pinch on her thighs. Her Santa Muerte swung in the distance. She searched for the bony hands of the lady that she loved, straining her eyes to the vast green leaves that hung over her lady's shroud as if to embrace her, as if to make an offering for safe passage to a place they wanted to go to.

de la found her Holy Death's hands in the garden, glowing white in the gray sky torched with shades of pink, and she felt her panties becoming like that frayed balloon ribbon in the dim of her office. She was a doctor. She knew such things. There was no need for her to shiver because her skin was warm and the leather seat under her was warm and wet with her sweat, like she was seeping into soil. She put her hand inside herself and opened herself, that thing she gave to her love on every night like this.

Tiny maggots moved like rosary beads on her hand. They became nervous things, curving like the moon that shone over her belly at night, and she knew that her lover was a fake lord indeed, and that night she would turn him out from her house and forbid him to ever come back, but then, just then, she could see him walking amongst the cold dead bodies in the hospital, finding the brown girl with the red ribbon in her hair, her skin seeped out of her hospital gown, paper blue, he inside her and growing and shaking like the flowers of the snow in the garden.

# IT SEAMS

JONNY'S FATHER carried his sewing kit into the afterlife.

Jonny's father wanted to make Jonny's mother a ghost dress from the bones and feathers of birds that had stopped breathing. He found the five tiny bird corpses lying still in the mouths of gutter ways, their feathers like blotches of blue and red and yellow paint. There was a small slip of paper wrapped on the wing of each bird and each of these papers said,

*An offering. A dress for our beloved doctor.*

The birds decided to give just enough bodies to make one dress. The thread from Jonny's father's sewing kit wasn't a proper match for the feathers on the bird, but he plucked them off their bodies anyway, the pull of the feathers a pain to no one but him.

Jonny's father found his beloved shivering with sweat in the hospital garden, the leaves of the trees lapping over her shoulder blades, the dark of her hair, only ribbons on her face. He laced the feathers of the birds around her hips that were like sharp blades jutting out to the sky and it was only then that she stopped her trembling. She looked around the circle of her, and he fell in love with the new radio fuzz that was now her body, but somehow he knew it only looked this way to him, to his dead eyes.

She saw that he had his sewing kit in the nook of his arm, the spools of threads peeking out of the basket like eyes and the needles floating like chinampas.

*I want to make my own dress,* she told him, looking straight in his eyes, a thing she never did when he was living. A look straight in her lover's eye scared her more than anything in the world. His body had been always a sideways glance, a turning over of skin, his shoulder a mountaintop turning in the sun that crept through the window blinds, when their bodies came tangled in the morning time.

*You made so many dresses for me and I always watched when you did it. They're all still hanging in my closet. Jonny says I should give them away, that you wouldn't be mad if did this. But I still keep them. I smell them to find the stink of you, but it's fading. Don't you think I know how to do it? Don't you think I know how to make a dress?*

She stepped over to the leaves that fell at Santa Muerte's feet, only half her body trembling then.

*I'm afraid for you, love,* he told her. *This thread will show you other things, things you may not feel ready to see yet. I know what he did to your body.*

He handed her the sewing basket and there was the shock of the wood in her palms, the rough bundle of branches, the parting gift of her ghost lover.

DE LA O spent all night sewing the dress, holding the corset to her own bones, using her own body as a mannequin. The thread glimmered when it was pulled through the fabric, the curtains over her kitchen window touching the breeze, the breeze passing over her shoulder blade, the needle rising and falling. She tried to remember what she did with her husband's sewing machine. She had packed it sideways in a box, the parts of it tossed in like they were sleeping, the cord wrapped around its neck. She didn't want it in the house any more, but she couldn't remember where she had put it.

The dress pulled her breasts together tightly, exposing them like twin moons, the fabric a curtain to her feet, her hips a sky. She still had the fragment of the first dress her husband had tried to make her in the garden and the tiny feathers shook in her hands. They were stitched with precision because he had sewn them together. The thread glimmered. She hung the feathers in the kitchen window. They would always speak back to her. She could hear the sound of feet coming up the sidewalk. The doctors and nurses and hospital administrators made a happy shroud in the night, coming to meet in her kitchen. She felt their murmur of voices in her spinal cord and her dress gripped her thighs as an offering.

# YOUR SCARS ARE A SPECTACLE

MY MOTHER, Marcrina worked as a nurse in Santa Muerte Hospital before The Generales had it shut down. She worked on the neonatal floor and some nights my father would take me to visit her, but I wasn't allowed in the nursery. I was only able to stand at the glass window and watch my mother, a blonde doll in pastel scrubs rocking babies in a plastic container, masks over their new eyes, the bright light an intrusion, a probe to their skin, new and shivering. My mother would always wave to me and smile weakly because the nights took their toll on her, but her eyes were always calm, joyful and full-moon slanted, black-lined with makeup that she pulled from the tiny pot that sat on top her vanity.

My mother had been afraid to join the protests because she didn't want to lose her job at the hospital since she hated to ask my father for money. She had, however, deemed it a worthy cause, and spoke about it with my father and I whenever she had the opportunity. She pulled fliers and newsletters out of her pockets while we ate dinner, and she shushed us to silence when the early morning news covered the protests.

I was always troubled by the scar that ran from my mother's pinky to her wrist. My father told me about the about the scar one night when she was at work.

When she had just started interning at the hospital, a patient in her delirium had grabbed an injection needle out of her hand and etched the line there on her skin. The woman's baby had just died and my mother forgave her for doing this. *I'm only telling you this story, so you won't ask her about it,* he told me. *She doesn't like to talk about it. It was a rough way to be initiated into the hospital.*

As the protests went on, my mother couldn't keep herself away and she joined her friends. All these protests led to The Generales shutting down the hospital. They said that the protests had become a spectacle and it was an embarrassment to everyone. One official called it "a fire that needs to be held under water" in one of the newspapers. For my family it was different. My mother and father knew that there was something that had taken over the hospital.

My mother's scar was just the start of them knowing. Nurses and doctors and administrators were being asked to cheat on their care to the poor and many of them refused to. They marched outside of City Hall, holding candles shaped like thorny roses and corn husks, the flames flickering and then dissipating into an echo of silence and the soft blur of street lamps. They marched on their days off from work because they didn't want to strike. They didn't want to leave their sick and their living alone to die. City Hall was a blue building shaped like a dome in the sky and my mother became one of the serpents that hissed under it, asking for answers that they just wouldn't give. Downtown was a flock of grey buildings, but City Hall has always been that blue menace in the clouds.

It was on a Sunday afternoon when all the lights went out in the hospitals. The medicine in IVs ceased to drip, heart beats turned to drum beats and then to zero. The clatter of moans was a quartet laced with blood and urine and sweat and cotton swabs of alcohol. Some patients were transported in vans to hospitals outside of the valley and some were left in the dark expanse of the walls, living tombs, clinging on uniformed bodies, nursed by candle light, trying to make it to the day scene. Some of the sick stood up and walked out and walked alone on the streets because they had nothing left to do. That very morning, the day the lights went out at the hospitals, my mother read her own cards and drew the one that said water.

# *D*ELIVER THE DEAD

MY MOTHER DELIVERED a dead baby the night before her crying jags came. This baby's mother was a young woman who lived in an apartment next to the railroad tracks off of Clinton and Blackstone Avenue. The woman wanted to give birth sitting in her favorite chair. When my mother arrived, the woman was sitting on her balcony knitting a green blanket that looked like sea kelp sprouting from in between her legs. The blanket was supposed to be for her living daughter, she said. Now it would be for her dead daughter. The woman's skin felt warm like water when my mother wrapped the tourniquet around the woman's arm and the needle went into the skin.

My mother made pomegranate tea for the woman and held it to her lips as they shivered in dark shades of pink like roses rotting on their stem. The woman's knees came apart, and the girl came out bluish and blooming and they wrapped her in the blanket her mother made for her. The woman wanted many pictures because the child's father was in the military and would not be able to see the baby at all. The sky outside was a pinkish hue and hung over the bare window and then it began to rain a light mist and my mother, Marcrina thought the sky must have looked like the insides of that baby and there was no baby crying, just a mother and the slow tug of her womb and her eyes.

MY MOTHER WALKED home in the mist, faded to dusty pink and then blue, the color of an azure stone she had tucked away in her vanity drawer as a child. She felt the money in the pocket of her bag and rubbed it between her fingers, as if she could make a tiny fire in the bag. There was a bar of black soap that she had bought at the market for her grandson, and as she passed the cemetery, she put the bag to her face and smelled the thick black slab. She had a quick wish, that the bag was plastic and she could pull it over her mouth and suffocate herself. That baby she had just birthed was warm, much warmer than any of the sick babies she had held at the hospital, but she was not alive, just warm like a petal hanging low and burning in the sun. She wondered if the baby would get her own plot in the cemetery. Most mothers paid her extra to bury their children, but this mother said she'd take care of the matters of her dead on her own.

When my mother got home to the apartment, she undressed and lay naked on her bed. On her nightstand, there was a piñata bird that her grandson had made for her when he had first learned to talk and take directions. She took the black soap from her purse and laid the bird on it and she thought she heard the bird cooing, lifting its neck, so that the notes became louder and the smell of the soap became more intense, wrapping itself around the mist that crept in through her window screen, the fragrance of the black soap reminded her of a little white church on a hill, a place she had gone as a girl.

The bird began to flap its wings and made its way towards the ceiling fan on her bedroom ceiling, whirring in between the blades and the cool air that spat on her and the bird, the flapping was a rhythm, a tiny drum song that she would never forget. She could hear her grandson's radio playing from his room and the washing machine spinning in the laundry room below our apartment. She heard brown children playing in the courtyard of the apartment complex, she could hear the green in the trees, she could hear the sun beat, and she could hear the cars on the street, and she began to cry and cry and cry tears that felt like needles and blades.

# PARKSIDE AND TEARDROPS

THERE ARE people that say my mother's tears sound like the large black cats that had left the valley long time ago. Others say that they sound like the rushing of water in a river and still others say they sound like heavy rain falling to puddles on concrete. To Nico, his grandmother's crying was like a drum because he heard it louder than anyone in the valley.

When The Generales came to take my mother away, our apartment had become a shallow green pool of water, and the stairway to our apartment had become a waterfall. The children had taken to climbing the waterfall in reverse and then sliding down, their mothers screaming up at the Lopez apartment because their children's clothes were getting ruined. *Our children*, they said, *are being ruined by Marcrina's tears*. Their children didn't want to do their chores or read books or go on picnics in the park. All they wanted to do was play in the tears of Marcrina Lopez.

If Nico was in a good mood, he'd laugh at them and sit on the balcony and play a baby guitar that his grandmother had bought him on a trip to LA. My mother had spent the day drinking cheap margaritas, and Nico had spent the day drinking Mexican soda pop and eating bacon-wrapped hot dogs from many different street vendors, and they had become so delirious from the eating and drinking that they had both passed out in their motel room, the swap cooler blasting the sweat on their sharp pink cheeks and their small brown necks. My mother had made the trip to get more supplies for birthing babies and Nico had begged to tag along. *Grandma, what do you call a birthday for a dead baby? They're not being born really. Are they called "Not Born Days?* Marcrina never gave her grandson an answer.

I WAS WORKING at the park when The Generales came to take my mother away, and Nico called my cell phone and got no answer. He begged the officials to take him too, and he said that he would go wherever his grandmother was going, but they left him there, and the waterfall from her tears turned to a small trail of mist in minutes. He went to my mother's room and found a wand of black sage in the cubby hole of her medicine desk and put the wand in a pot that she had bought from a thrift store years ago.

The pot had a crooked clown face on it and it was the first time he noticed that it was so poorly painted and he wondered why my mother had even bought the pot at all. He decided that she must have bought the pot because she like the muted colors, the pinks, the purples, the blues, and the yellows that dripped one on top of the other like candle wax. Like birthday candles on cake, he thought.

He had seen such beauties at the panadería around the corner, but now it wasn't time to be mourning beauty. It was time to burn this pot of sage. He went to the patio and lit one end of the sage wand and set it in the pot and wound his body around in circle, marveling at the dark of his arms. He hadn't realized that he's been spending so much time in the sun. Three of the neighbor women were sitting in the courtyard shaving their son's heads because the children had been getting lice from swimming all day in the communal pool.

"What the hell are you doing?" I called out from below. My son's face was like tarnished stone, coming alive at the sight of me.

"My mom called me. They took her to a clinic and have some doctors looking at her. I told those idiots that they better get her out of there fast. Before the sun goes down."

"Why'd they take her there? When there's nothing even wrong with her?"

He set the bowl on the balcony ledge and saw the women and the little girls hold their noses.

"You're burning the wrong color. White is for cleansing. Black is for if you want to have dreams."

"It's all I could find in grandma's room."

"Maybe it's a good thing. You'll need something to help you sleep tonight."

# ᴹARCRINA MUÑECA

MARCRINA DEMANDED that The Generales make her a beautiful house for her exile. A tiny house, but a strong-built house with a pond and ducklings in the back. It only took six days for them to do it because a hipster in San Francisco had revived catalogue houses again. All The Generales had to do was pull the pieces of her house out of a truck and put them together like a paint-by-the-numbers set. I wondered how The Generales would pick the spot where my mother would live. I imagined they would take a map with many lines like bones and tissue and veins in a body and one of them would close their eyes and point at the map with their finger and pick a spot for Marcrina. But this was a home for a woman who cried every single night, and so, my mother was sent to the cenote in Parkside. My mother also demanded a dog, a girl dog, one that they would rescue from the streets. There were few healthy dogs in the city. The animal clinic came in less frequently than the clinics for people and Marcrina argued that dogs would one day become extinct in Cenote City. They brought her a chubby white dog with fur like a lamb, its back spattered with grey like clouds. She named the dog Lucy, so that she could be the namesake of many, so she could inherit their strength and have a long life. Alex was appointed as one of her guards and he said, *take the dog for morning walks around the cemetery down the road. It'll be good for you.* She liked when Alex said that the cemetery was like a dress because railroad tracks ran through it like a zipper and flowers sprouted out of the ground like buttons. All of the tiny trinkets left on the grave, paper kites and pinwheels and stuffed clowns made the cemetery sway and then undress when the occasional rain would come down in the fall and in the springtime.

My mother watched as Alex waited for her at the neck of the cemetery, its old grey road running out of it like a tongue. And when she saw that he wasn't watching her so closely, she took her letters, tiny triangles of green paper and she stuck them in the same hole at the grave of the Resendez family, a family that built an immense daffodil garden around their dead. The family has long died out, but The Generales kept up the spot because it was another garden the tourists liked to look at after watching my mother at the cenote. When she was certain that Alex couldn't see her, she pulled out the metal cup for flowers and stuck her letters in the ground and prayed that the worms wouldn't excrete too much blood or feces on the paper, so that her writing would become illegible. She had spent months training Lucy not to bark loudly when they ventured out. The dog looked like a little ghost lamb, tapping her long brush-like tail on each and every stone that she walked upon. My mother never took stock in the notion that she shouldn't step on graves. She believed that footsteps were a blessing for the dead because somehow they would know that they were still attuned to the earth and the living.

# GIFTS FOR XIBALBA

I HAD ONLY BEEN to the cenote once in my life and it was my father who brought me here. It was the last time I saw him. He had packed us a picnic lunch and drove us out to the cenote in his pick-up truck and he was blasting "Cowboys to Girls" on his stereo. Every time that song got to the part about shooting them up, I would make my fingers like a gun and pull the trigger. That day I decided to play at shooting birds and tree branches that hung down like the arms of giants, the misty air making my father's bearded face like fuzz, and when a tree branch softly scraped the top of my head, I knew that I felt pleasure and fear in equal measure, and I let out a scream because the tree felt good on me, and my father laughed, as if he knew that I wasn't scared at all.

My father's skin was much lighter than mine and he had slick black hair with no bend. I don't know what his hair looks like now. I thought that he looked like a movie star then, the kind of movie star that changes his last name to one that doesn't sound Spanish. He had a gentle laugh and always smelled like pricey cologne and whisky.

He laid out a blanket for us to sit on and told me all about the cenote as we ate lunch. Cold sandwiches wrapped in comic book paper and fruit punch for me and wine for him. I told him that I refused to ride home with him if he was going to be drunk, and he just laughed at me and said, *Ok, I'll just leave you here then to fend for yourself.* He told me about the history of the cenote. How when his family first came here from Texas, they would throw things in the cenote as offerings to Xibalba, how they did this to win favor and blessings, to protect them from any negative energy that other families would wish open them. There are many people that will wish you harm if you are successful, he told me. I wasn't really sure how he thought his family was a great success, but I let my father talk on. He told me my mother's family would come to the cenote as well.

All the families came to the cenote until one day they begun to lose their faith in old ways and then the cenote was just a waterhole with no purpose. The trees began to sway as my father told me these stories, and I reached up and grabbed a branch and pulled it to the earth like it was a quill pen and gently wrote my name in the dirt. A bird flew over the middle of the cenote and squawked at the sky, as if it knew there was something below, something only the bird could see.

The bird had blue and green and yellow feathers and along the edge of its wings there was red feather, making the wings look like they had been stitched on with red thread. The bird kept squawking and squawking at the sky and my father kept talking, but his words were fading away, like black-and-white TV snow. I began to wonder if my father had accidentally poured me wine because I was beginning to feel sleepy, and I had once overheard a woman at the hospital talk about how wine always made her sleepy. I kept my eye on the bird and the bird looked as if it was admiring its own reflection in the water that was far far below it. My father pulled out a small satchel filled with crushed flowers petals and stems and handed it to me.

*Here, he said, Feed the bird.*

*Birds don't eat flowers. They eat breadcrumbs.*

*Feed the bird. You'll see, Lune. Why don't you ever believe me?*

This was the first time that I ever saw my father look sad and I felt embarrassed, not for him, but for myself. He began to pack our things carefully in the basket and whistle softly. The sky was shifting to a pale pink hue and there were roly poly insects crawling up my legs. Instead of screaming, I brushed them off, trying to hum a tune to match my father's whistle. My father brushed his blue-black hair in the side view mirror of his truck and played a pretend flute with his left hand. His wedding ring didn't shine in the pale light that shone through the trees.

*Don't you miss living here, dad?* I asked him.

I felt myself whisper to the cenote. *One day, I will have my own child and leave this city*, I told myself. As I walked over to the cenote, I began to rub flower petals in tiny circles between my fingertips, then tossed them into the sky. The flowers were blue and they made a circle around the bird, who hovered at the mouth of the cenote like a bruise. The bird looked at me with its black eyes and then its tiny body fell down into the cenote, the flowers like stars like rain, my own mouth eating the sky in an O of constellation.

# *J*ONNY EX OH AND THE HOSPITAL GARDEN

JONNY TOLD people that he was born in a murderous place on the other side of the valley. He grew up hearing his mother and the ghost of his father whispering in corners, their shadows only recognizable when he was close enough to hear them. His mother was one of the city's most respected doctors, until she decided to turn over the hospital and its secrets. Once his mother took him to work when he was thirteen years old and let him roam the hospital by himself. The exterior of the hospital looked like green selenite stones lined up next to each other, like one thin twin birthing the other. The sun was shining brightly, but the wind cut sharp, happy blades on his neck because he had just got his hair cut shorter than usual.

The children at school were always impressed when Jonny told them that his mother was a doctor, but now that they were in the hospital, there were many women and men like her, and he felt disappointed at this realization. His mother always wore blue green scrubs the color of an ocean tide that Jonny had seen many times. His mother and ghost father took him to the beach often because they had built a house there. As he thought of the beach house, he went and sat on a stone bench in the hospital garden. He had expected to see a flower bed, but instead, there were so many flowers that he couldn't even see the soil, only buds coming up the way blood rose from his own fingertip like a pinprick. He took out his phone and tried to draw a picture of his family's beach house.

The beach house had been called unusual because it had been built from black brick and the bricks weren't staggered like red bricks usually are, but laid one on top of the other like a stack of cards. Jonny used his pinky to draw the tiny thin lines between the bricks and the large stained glass panels on either side of the front door. His mother had chosen to make the windows orange and green because those were the colors of her favorite cat's fur and eyes, and since the cat had passed into Xibalba, the windows were a memorial to his earthly body and spirited nature.

"A cat on a beach house! My mother is crazy!" Jonny said out loud as he drew the sloping curve of the cat's tail and spiked the ends like razor blades.

He heard a woman laughing from the other side of the garden. She had a black lunch bag that rolled up the top and played a tune and had yellow lights that flicked on and off like a siren. She had long bleached blonde hair and brown eyes that slanted into half moons. Her voice was calm like water.

"I'm sorry, I'm not laughing at you. I was just thinking about something funny," the woman said, covering her mouth with her tiny hand. She had a thick ropey scar on her hand that made him shiver because he thought it was beautiful.

Jonny began to draw the sand around the beach house with digital brown ink and he hung the moon and the stars so low over the house that they looked like a baby mobile, so he made it so they would hover around in the picture, and he made the waves crash against the brick of the house and roll back in the clouds like puppets in a show.

"Are you visiting someone? Are you here with your family?" The woman asked him.

He squinted to read her name tag. *Marcrina Lopez.* He wondered how you said a name like that. He wrote La Luna inside the half moon in his picture and sunk the moon in the tide.

"I'm here with my mom. My mom brought me. I don't know why."

"So, your mom's visiting someone here?"

"My mom delivers babies. She is a doctor here."

"Really. I help take care of the babies. But, I'm not a nurse just yet. I'm still doing my internship. Maybe I know your mom. What's her name?"

"Sylvia de la O."

"Dr. de la O? She's been really nice. Some of the other doctors, not so much. I'm just an intern, so you know. I'm still studying to be a baby nurse. Most of them don't respect me yet."

Jonny didn't really know what an intern was, but he was too embarrassed to ask her.

"Are you drawing a picture?"

"How did you know?"

"You just look really serious right now. Besides, my daughter used to have one of those phones. She bugged and bugged me for it until I finally gave in."

"I got this at the video store in Tower."

"Yeah, they were always trying to buy my daughter's when we'd go in there to rent movies. Can I see your picture?"

As Marcrina walked over, the flowers seemed to sway in her path. She smelled like rubbing alcohol and like the water and the moon. He handed her his phone, the picture flickering and the waves crashing louder and louder.

"This is beautiful," she said, thumbing the signature on the bottom of the screen. Signed in digital blood. "This is beautiful, Jonny Ex Oh."

# THE TEQUILA TEXT OF LOVE

THE NIGHT after the racetrack quinceañera, Stevie decided to profess his love for Professor Mundo via text message. Most of those close to him knew he was in love with his clown teacher because he told us so. He talked about his clown teacher all the time. He had invited me and Yoli and Carlo over to his apartment for Piper's Pizza. He asked us to bring the booze, which we were always happy to supply. We ordered music videos from a TV program called "The Rox" with his ATM card. Stevie usually just waited for other people to buy songs, but he had just gotten a windfall of money from mariachi and pizzeria paychecks, and he was in a generous mood. When a person called in to order a song on "The Rox," their name would appear on the TV screen and so, every time we saw Steven or Stevie or Sanchez on the screen, we all drank a shot of tequila. Stevie asked us to bring white tequila because it went down smooth and because Professor Mundo said in class once that white tequila was the best.

Yoli had made herself a new green striped pencil skirt and matching shirt. It fit dangerously. She had just dyed her hair jet-black and there was dye drip on the back of her shirt, but it sort of looked like Ash Wednesday ash or a cool trick, so no one even brought it to her attention. She brought candles in pink, yellow, and green cauldrons that she'd bought at the general store because we had planned to have a séance to contact her grandmother who had strayed from her women's club, The League of Mexican Mayhem, during a nighttime excursion. She had gotten lost and died in a corn maze on a ranch just outside of the city the year before. The people on the ranch had been in such a frenzy to find her that they kept getting lost and begged The Generales to bring in a helicopter to fly over and find her. They refused, and by the time the ranch hands found her, her grandmother was doing a death tango with a dilapidated scarecrow piñata, a paper prince that had been pulled from the attic and propped in the maze every year. If only piñatas could talk, everyone said that night. Maybe he could have helped the woman find her way out.

YOLI'S GRANDFATHER had a glass casket built and kept her there for seven days because he said that's how long it took his god to make the paradise that earth once was and seven days was also the exact number of days it took for his wife to give birth to all of her children. She had hated the hospitals and was glad to see them shut down because they made child bearing unbearable. And also, seven was the number of dwarves in Snow White and the Seven Dwarves, and that had always been her favorite fairy tale to tell their daughters. And that fairy tale had a glass casket too.

Yoli wanted to contact her grandmother and ask her what she really died of.

"She died of fright. Everyone knows that!" Carlo said as he tried to pour equal amounts of tequila in each of the beakers that they used for shot glasses. The beakers had been hand-me-down gifts from Marcrina's old medical bag with the promise that they had been sterilized and smudged and were free of any poison or lingering dead baby spirit.

"I don't buy that whole she-died-of-fright bullshit. My grandma was too real to die that way. My grandma was a G."

Stevie lowered the TV so that the music went from a drum to a hum and he took his seat in the breakfast nook where the others were sitting and waiting for him. I was wearing a low cut top and I could tell he admired my breasts even though he didn't want to touch them. I had always told him that I was proud to be out of my twenties because I hated being called "Miss" at the grocery store and I told him I felt like an older sister to him and to Marco. Not any wiser, but more jaded. He noticed that my hands were full of nicks and ink from clearing away letters and trinkets from the cenote. I was wearing a yellow blouse with oversized Pachuca pants, crisp at the crease and grey like smoke. The incense on the tabletop burned a hello. It was getting dark in the tree house because the sun was falling. We could hear a banjo playing in the main house and mad crickets violin on the window sill.

"Are we going to hold hands?" I asked Yoli.

Yoli had her eyes closed and her coral-lipsticked lips pursed like a 1940's pin-up girl.

"I thought we were going to take a shot."

"No, we'll take a shot once we've made contact with Yoli's Gma."

"I don't know about this. Necromancy is fancy fancy," Carlo said. "I don't think I'm good at this stuff."

"This is notttttt necromancy! Here, let's take each other's hands!"

"Lune, light another cone," Yoli said to me.

"No, my eyes are burning. I think I'm allergic."

"Close your eyes."

"Grandma! Grandma! Can you hear us?"

Even though Stevie was supposed to be thinking about Yoli's grandmother, he was thinking about Professor Mundo and his goatee, which he thought to be his most handsome asset. He began to pray that Professor Mundo would never get old because then he might not find him attractive any more. Professor Mundo had given him his phone number when he started the project for the clown fair exhibition and he planned to use it. He just wanted the séance to be over, so that he could text him.

A giant slotted spoon hanging on the wall fell off and knocked over Marco's tequila shot.

"Damn it. This stuff's not cheap, you know."

"She knows. Grandma only used to drink the happy hour stuff."

The banjo in the main house grew louder and Stevie put his hands out to me and Carlo. Carlo's hand was in a loose grip so I made sure to hold on tight. He could feel the spikes in my rings, but they felt good on his skin, and made him think of Professor Mundo and the text that he would send him.

Yoli's grandmother snuffed out two of the candles and made the dishes in the sink rattle, but she wouldn't talk.

"Shouldn't we be using a Ouija board?"

"No, Ouija boards are for YTs!"

"Not true, sir. Another shot for grandma."

Yoli took each beaker and dipped the rims in a clay bowl filled with pink Himalayan salt, filled the beakers, and passed the first one to Stevie.

"You look pained, friend. You need this."

Stevie took the shot fast. It stung his throat. The smell of the tequila made him think of the last time he had been at the clinic. He was getting his blood drawn and the nurse had wrapped the tourniquet too tight, but the swab of alcohol felt like a breeze on his skin. The nurse was black and had hair the color of the cenote, it was a bluish green and smelled like coconut. He took out his phone and texted Professor Mundo,

*Are you down? BTW, this is Steven Sanchez. Your clown student.*

"Are you going to the cenote tonight, Lune?" Stevie asked me.

Yoli opened her eyes. They were blood-shot and lacked weeping.

Yoli said, "Let's go. Let's all go."

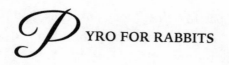

# PYRO FOR RABBITS

THERE WERE MORE guards at the cenote because it was Friday night. The strobe lights were flashing pink and green because those were Marcrina's favorite colors. Marcrina's wails could be heard above the music. The song went,

> *And the music is a loud drum*
> *And I'm not his Pocahontas baby anymore.*

There was a handsome taco guy grilling asada and buche next to the duckling pond. He was wearing a pink tank top with a blue haired mermaid on it, her torso skeletal and glowing in the dark. The ducklings ran for the bits of tortilla the children threw at them, weaving in and out of the crowd that made a horseshoe shape around the perimeter of the cenote. Nico was sweeping the patio, while a girl talked to him, blowing bubbles from her syringe shaped necklace. Nico smiled up at me when I walked up to him and pulled the broom from his hands.

"I told you, let them take care of this. They shouldn't be asking you to clean."

"We can't wait around for The Generales to do everything for us," Nico said. He put the broom down and walked away with the girl with the bubble necklace who took his hand as they made off for the trees. Yoli and Stevie had set a blanket out in front of the cenote and were passing their notebook back and forth to each other. They'd been writing to each other in a notebook since they were kids. They had been in the same kindergarten class and had been so shy that the school began to pull them out of class as a pair to work with a tutor. The tutor gave them a notebook that they would share and asked them to write about all the things they wanted to say about their day. They'd been writing to each other ever since.

I've seen them write in many different notebooks. Once they fill a new notebook, Stevie buys another one. Stevie keeps all the notebooks under his bed so that no one else can open them and read them. That night at the cenote, they were writing in a bright red book with a skull on the cover.

The guards began to filter out tourists at the cenote, so that they could let in the tourists still waiting at the gate. One of the guards went up to my friends and tried to escort them out, but then Alex went up and stopped them. Alex looked over at me and smiled and I couldn't help but smile back at him. The taco guy switched on a lamp at his stand and the night blared bright over Alex's narrow shoulders. He wasn't wearing a shirt under his white leather moto vest and I noticed that he had hickies on his neck and chest. They looked like little purple flowers on his brown skin.

He walked over to me with his paper plate of tacos and got so close I could smell lemon and cilantro. He smiled at me and I felt the hot breeze on my legs. I have always adored Alex's teeth. He has the most beautiful teeth I have ever seen on a man.

"That's your friend, right. He's a clown?" He pointed to Stevie.

"He's almost A Clown of Everything."

"I'm looking to hire a clown to play a practical joke."

"Why are you asking me about it? Go talk to him. He's really nice to talk to."

"Maybe I just wanted an excuse to talk to you."

ALEX'S practical joke was to pretend that a child of The Generales had died at the cenote. Stevie had learned how to put children in a coffin and make them disappear and then reappear again. We didn't have a coffin handy, so I let them use the trunk that my mother had turned upside down and used as a coffee table.

Alex announced an impromptu magic show at the cenote. At the stroke of midnight, Stevie, the almost Clown of Everything would perform a miraculous feat. All that Stevie needed was a child volunteer from the cenote audience. Alex had to yell this at the cenote audience very loudly so that they could hear him over Marcrina's crying. Stevie stood quietly at the cenote and let Alex scour the crowd for a child of The Generales. I only wanted him to make a little cash. Alex had already tucked a wad of bills in the pocket of Stevie's shorts. He found a blonde teenage boy to go into the luggage case. He folded his arm into an X as he went down. The cenote crowd buzzed and began to film the magic show on their phones. A woman from the crowd yelled, *How can a clown put on a magic show? He's not a magician!* Yoli, yelled, *He's better than a magician. He's an almost Clown of Everything.*

As if Yoli was his cue, Stevie pulled a balloon out of his pocket and began to blow it and when it burst, it burned red pyrotechnics in the air. Alex and Yoli and Carlo began to wave for the crowd to move back. The smoke snaked through the crowd and mingled with the sizzle of the taco grill. Stevie opened the trunk with one long swoop of his arm. The boy wasn't inside. The crowd cheered and cheered and Stevie slammed the case shut. He pulled a tiny orange out of his pocket and pulled the peel back and a bird flew out and began to hover over the crowd and then flew over the gate and into the dark. The crowd roared. I felt the hot breeze on my neck and the onions on the grill made my stomach ache. There were yellow pyrotechnics that made the shapes of daisies at the exact moment that Marcrina let out her loudest teardrop into the cenote. Then there were black pyrotechnics in a form that I couldn't make out because the sky was so dark. A few children began to yell out, *Rabbit! Rabbit. That thing's a rabbit!* The fire was indeed a rabbit that turned into white smoke with pink eyes. Stevie opened the trunk to show that the boy had returned. But the boy hadn't come back. The trunk was empty.

# TREE SPELLS

WE SEARCHED FOR THE BOY, my mother's tears still falling into the cenote. Most of the tourists had scattered, afraid that they'd be disappeared next. They left the ground littered with candy wrappers and paper plates. The taco grease lingered in the air like clouds. Nico found the blonde boy under the trees just as my mother's cries began to stop and the morning birds had begun to chirp in their holes. Nico said that the boy was sleeping peacefully on his back, as if he was floating up a river. His arms at his side. Nico shook the boy, so that he would wake up, and the boy laughed out loud and yelled at the trees, running and tripping and flipping off the sky. The sun was pink with the promise of a hot day, but then there was only the smoke that had settled from the pyrotechnics and the ducks that padded their feet on the earth. Stevie sat at the mouth of the cenote and gave it praise for the very first time.

# THE RED LINE

HIS NAME WAS JONNY. He had been going to college outside of the valley, but his mother asked him to work in the mobile clinics, just for the summer. She had promised.

"What color is your clinic?" I asked.

All of the medical clinics were painted different colors and serviced different sections of Cenote City, running through the streets, looking for sick people. This only happens on Tuesdays. Whenever one of the tourists asks me why they come on Tuesdays, I never have a good answer to give them. No one has ever told me. Stevie and Carlo always hated that it was on Tuesday because if something was ailing them, they had to miss Taco Tuesday at Bat/house Bar and they thought that was a shame because Yoli works there on that night and always pours the liquor heavy, even though she isn't supposed to.

"You can catch me on the red line," Jonny said.

Storylandia was empty, except for us three. Me and Nico and Jonny.

Nico began to climb up Jack's beanstalk and I noticed that the bottom of his jeans were ripped and caked with dirt. I had been noticing how short he was, but stocky in stature, his shoulder wide like his father's, a man he has never once seen before. A young man who I am losing from my memory. He can only be conjured by a jukebox and tequila shots and bright blue soap. Without these things, Nico's father is as dead to me as the babies that my mother used to pull from women's bodies.

Jonny told me that children would be invited to the clinic fundraiser and that's why he wanted to have it at Storylandia.

"I haven't been here in years. It looks so much smaller now," he said.

"It probably won't be here much longer. The Generales want to shut it down. They already make enough money from the zoo."

Jonny leaned against a rosebush and I was embarrassed for him to see it because the petals looked tinged with rust, the way a bathroom sink does when the water drips too long. I walked over and thumbed the petals of one drooping rose.

"They are dying," I told him. I began to pull petals of the rose, as if it would make the entire bush of flowers bloom like new. It was too late. But then it felt like Jonny was reading my mind.

"It's OK that they're dead. I've always liked the smell of dying flowers."

"There's a bunch of dead shit in here," Nico called out, his voice a tiny echo.

As we walked over, Jonny brushed a few steps before me and I saw that his hair wasn't brown, but black. When I was a little girl, my father told me that there was no such thing as black hair or black eyes because that was unnatural. He said that black wasn't a color, but the absence of color. He said that wearing the color black would protect me from those that would wish me harm. No, Jonny's hair was not black, after all. When we got to the amphitheater inside Storylandia, Nico was standing on the stage, his arms outstretched and his eyes closed. I've always wondered what me and my friends look like when we're doing a séance or calling the corners, but now, thanks to Nico, I know we look like beautiful dead things. The amphitheater is made of brown brick and each brick has orange circles and squares and triangles on them.

"They used to do puppet shows here. You know, minstrel shows. Horror shows. They used to do those here. They had movie nights. They did them after the park was closed to the public," Jonny told me.

Nico opened his eyes wide and pulled a piece of pink chalk out of the pocket of his hoodie.

"How do you know that? Who told you about that?"

"My mother did. She used to come to them. She brought me once. Right before they closed all the hospitals."

I walked along the seats of the amphitheater, and I could feel Jonny walking behind me. I imagined what it would be like to walk on the seats barefoot. The scorch of the sun like a flame and it felt good there. I liked that Jonny's black leather shoes had laces like worms. I wished that it could be nighttime, completely. I pretended that it was dark and that the amphitheater was lit by lanterns and gnats hummed around them like the bracelets on my wrists. I wished it was night. Me and Jonny walked in a half-circle like someone had cut the moon in half and set it in the amphitheater, so that it would always be night there. I stopped right before I got on the stage and it was so suddenly, that Jonny bumped behind me. I could smell his pomade again and it smelled like it glowed, the swirl of his black hair was a real thing. Jonny's hair was black, after all. Nico had vanished again and was nowhere to be seen.

"Some people were against bringing kids to the shows, but my mom wanted me to know what was going on with the hospitals. I'm surprised you never came," Jonny said.

"I came here a lot when I was a kid," I told him, stepping onto the stage. My red patent leather shoes were slick and glimmering with dust. I turned around and looked at Jonny, who was still standing on the stone, the beanstalk rising high in the distance.

"I'm talking about here," Jonny said. I'm talking about the shows. Your mother is Marcrina Lopez.

# *B*LUE PLASTIC FLOWER
## (THE NIGHT SHOW)

THERE IS the tapping of feet and the soft glow of flashlights like polka dots coming from outside Storylandia and outside its theater, but the audience pays no mind to these things. There are always the small steps of park goers walking and running in circles outside of the place, even on a Tuesday night, when it's less busy than usual. Tonight is not play night, tonight is novela night.

*CAT IS fourteen years old and her room is adorned with star and planet stickers that she bought from quarter machines at the Fulton Mall. Cat's father touches her and tries to charm her at night. He runs his pale hand up her thigh and feels it shake there. She is grateful that he does nothing more than this. She used to love her father and now the sight of him makes her want to fly up to the moon in a hot air balloon. She tells all this to the moon as a promise. She'll get there someday. She is sick. She wants a good kind of love.*

"CAN LOVE REALLY MAKE YOU SICK?" Lune asks her mother. There are tree branches that are scraping the makeshift screen. The screen is a sheet that is made with hands and with love and is still spotted with the fingerprints of the people that made it. Lune sits knee-to-knee with another little girl she knows only as Snugz because her mother called her by that name right before the movie started.

ONE DAY *while walking through the Fulton Mall, Cat meets a boy that is just a few years older than her. He asks if he can sit next to her by the water fountain and they talk and talk about all kinds of things like books and taxidermy and the way that grapes freeze on the vines in the winter. The boy says he picks grapes in the summer. Birds fly in and out of the fountain and watch as Cat begins to fall in love with the boy and he falls in love with her in return. She tells the boy about flying to the moon. He says that he would be happy to go with her there. They walk together to the store fronts and stop when they came to a botanica. The boy asks her if she wants to have her cards read for the day. He will pay for it. Cat refuses because she is afraid of the death card. She is always afraid of a three card reading. They take each other's hands as she says death and they walk inside the store. The boy wants to buy her a blue plastic flower that lights up with batteries. The flowers are sticking out of a long brown barrel that holds bright red umbrellas with spikes on the end of them. Cat pulls an umbrella from the barrel and holds it to the boy's rib cage and he smiles at her. He touches the baby hairs that frame her face and she purrs like she's a lioness. The screen goes dark and Cat and the boy are in another place, a small hole in the ground that is ringed in trees, a tiny forest in the alleyway of the mall.*

THE MOTHER of Snugz puts her hand over the eyes of Snugz and the little girl squirms under ribbon of skin. Lune knows her own mother wants her to watch because she said that she would never hide anything from her, even if it hurts Lune on the inside. Lune watches the boy and girl kiss on the screen and their bodies stitch together in love. The girl is wearing a white cotton shirt sewn like a peasant blouse and black jeans that sit at her thick hips waiting for the boy to touch them. There are car doors shutting outside of Storylandia, and the birds are screeching softly from their zoo cages on the other side.

THE GIRL NAMED *Cat gives birth to her baby in a white hospital room with blue tiles on the wall. Cat and her love will fly away to the moon together with their baby. Her love is not allowed in the room with her. The doctors forbid it. Cat's father had paid them to do this. He waits for her in the hospital garden. The doctor cups his white hands over the baby's mouth, the baby's blue brown hands flail like ribbons spinning away. The girl named Cat has become a pair of half opened eyes that look blood flowered as if they were wrapped in lace. A nurse takes the baby to another room and gives the baby a bath. The baby cries and shivers. The baby is dressed in a black gown with a white string at the bottom. The nurse pulls the string and the baby kicks their legs under the gown.*

WHEN LUNE SEES the baby swaddled on the screen, it makes her think of her living mother and her grandmother who was long asleep in the ground. How they would say that a baby should always be covered from their head to their toes, so that they wouldn't catch cold, so that demons wouldn't come into their tiny bodies through their tiny eyes and their tiny throats and their tiny lungs. When the baby is handed over to a man in hospital scrubs, when the baby is taken away, down the hospital walls and through the leaves of the hospital garden, just past the teenaged father that does not see, Lune feels the cool breeze like a cold blade on the warm sweat on her neck. She hadn't even realized that the sweat was there until then.

*The hospital tells Cat that her baby is dead. They tell her that they will take care of everything. No need to worry. No need to worry her family. They will bury her dead. Her love waits for her in the hospital garden. All they need is her hand to sign the certificate, the ink is like the liquid that drips from her IV, the chill of alcohol is a numb thing on her nose, the bones of her dead baby, an echo in her skull. No drum beat, just an echo.*

The smell of pink and caramel popcorn bleeds the air and the screen goes black and is then dotted with tiny holes and shapes that blink in and out like eyes. Lune feels the little girl Snugz shake up against her and her tiny mouth buds against her lobe. "What happened to her baby?" Snugz asks her. And before Lune can answer, there is a flood of lights and feet that rush against them.

# ℬLOOD SONG FOR ORPHANS

THEY'D NEVER MISTAKE the red and blue lights for strobe lights or anything they would claim as joyful. The amphitheater had been packed with doctors and nurses and their children. Limbs trying to stay still in anticipation. If it had been a play night, black and brown actors would have been dressed like the dead. Hospital beds made from cardboard boxes and bright blue laundry baskets turned over and blankets made of construction paper. Hospital administrators would have had large and looming puppets twisted around their fingers, and there would be piñatas with large eyes and mouths twisted into shapes, dancing in fake fog.

The Generales tumbled into the theater like marbles, bright white flashlights, lights dotting the skin of the audience, the children crying out like birds. The Generales lined all the adults in the grassy patch that grew haphazardly outside the theater. The adults stood shoulder to shoulder like sticks and the children gathered in a circle on the grass. Some of the children trembled and some shivered despite the absence of heat while others scanned the sky for stars.

Lune was wearing a blue dress that ballooned on the grass and made her look smaller than she was. She took a small flute from her pocket and began to play it to calm the children who were coughing and rubbing their eyes and pulling out the grass with their tiny fists. And as she was playing, she turned to look at her mother, dressed in pink, her blonde hair blowing in the hot wind. The Generales took pictures of the adults with cameras that flashed and made a small spectacle in the dark. Lune imagined where those pictures would go, on a wall, small sheets of color, exposures of faces, hospital workers, the mothers and fathers of the children sitting in a circle. The officers made the children walk out of the Storylandia in a single file line into the parking lot. White chalk lines striped the lot like rib bones. Lune steadied her shoes on a white line, trying to keep balance.

The Concrete Carnival hovered in the distance. It was emptied of lights but the shadows of the machines were still recognizable. Lune tried to hear the clown music in the air, but she couldn't. Three shots rang out from Storylandia. Those gunshots made orphans that night. Some of the adults came running out of Storylandia grabbing at children, limbs of flesh trying to find their children. Only some of the mothers and fathers came for their children. Lune's mother found her and the orphans and they made their way off in the dark.

# ONE THOUSAND LITTLE STARS IN HIS MOUTH

WHEN MY FATHER told my mother he was leaving her, she had been one of the most active women in the protests against the hospital. He had been waiting to leave her, but he wanted to wait until she could make it on her own, until she had her own money and her own friends.

He told her that he was going to leave her on Christmas Eve. The morning before he told her, they had argued about an old Christmas box that my mother insisted on keeping. The box held a long-limbed elf and dried apple ornaments that were sewn to look like the faces of old Mexican women. All of their eyes had been chewed out by rats but my mother had insisted on keeping them and began to cry when my father had threatened to throw them away.

Christmas Eve, my mother was wearing a black silk dress and my father was wearing a black silk shirt that had been made by Dr. de la O's husband, who was a tailor. My mother had them made especially for the hospital garden party. She looked like a black river at the party, a brilliant black beetle when she walked through the leaves of the flowers, the silk in her dress rippled like liquid under the hot air that blew from the heaters, bits of silver swimming under the glow of lights. Blue lights braided with purple lights hung over them like a pendulum and the string of lights would only move when the band played a particularly slow song. My father danced with my mother that night. My mother's lips were painted over with oxblood, a gift from a patient, an old woman that had lived in New Mexico when she was a girl.

My father kissed my mother's lips and tasted the animal's blood and it tasted like one thousand little stars in his mouth. He didn't like the taste of it because it reminded him that she would never be his. That she would never really belong to him. He knew that he had been foolish to think that they would last, that their daughter would keep them together. My father thought of me, asleep under the Christmas tree in my black velvet gown and ribbon in my hair. He took a long breath of the cold foggy air to strengthen his resolve. The lights above him blinked on and off.

My mother and father danced and danced and other couples flew around them in circles, the violin sounding the loudest over from the band, a white Christmas tree towered over them, decked with hundreds of cuckoo clocks. The birds would emerge on the hour and sing their song. This city used to be called Flute. That was our city *then*. That was the hospital garden. My father whispered in my mother's ear, his voice on her neck. He was leaving her. It was Christmas. It was her gift. He wouldn't burden her anymore. She could be free now. He said. She could be committed to the cause. She could stay out until the early morning, the sky would bleed pink just for her, just like the mouth of that bird cooing in her other ear. He grabbed his love like a bracelet and told her to remember his words when she felt like she was lost.

He loved her completely. He would be gone before morning.

Dr. de la O asked if she could cut into their dance, her hot pink tequila lips cutting the cold sky in giggles and Lune's father obliged her. He only stayed a moment, long enough to see his wife's eyes stained, not with a deep shade like the oxblood, but another shade of blood. Her eyebrows were like thin puffs of smoke that might evaporate in the fog and the mist. She lay her head on de la O's shoulder and drowned. My father made his way out of the hospital garden as the band began to play a new song, as the hospital workers began to clink their glasses to a toast.

All of this was a disguise. A mask to hide their rebellion. A fistful of dust flung in the eyes of their enemies. The flowers bent low and tangled, their leaves specked all over with tiny red lights, like a million eyes, not bright enough for my father to see a clear path to where he was going, but not dark enough to turn back and stay with my mother. He thought he heard her call out to him, her voice as small and beautiful as it always was, but that fragment of her voice lay hooked inside the call of the cuckoo birds, glowing and shaking under the moonlight. My father knew what his wife was doing. She wanted to save the sick. He saw the good in it. He kept looking for more and more glow lights. He was just looking for a way out of the garden.

# THE DAFFODIL DRESS

THE SPRING after Lune's father left them, she found her mother in the backyard of their house, floating in a plastic baby pool, her dress blooming around her body like a daffodil. Lune had been to a birthday party in Storylandia. She began to scream and tried to pull her mother out of the water. The warmth of the water was a shock to her hands and it soaked her party dress, making the skin on her legs burn and itch. She clawed at her own skin with her nails, painted pink by her mother with care. If the clouds could bear witness to that afternoon, they would say that Lune was a swirl of ribbons and brown skin, her kneecaps scraped by the sea of grass, bluish green and bleating, not willing to give up their secrets.

Lune's screams were loud enough to bring the neighbors, to bring the ambulance, to bring the police, to bring Lune's father. The paramedic, a young woman with slanted eyes and bright hair administered CPR, while the next-door-neighbor clung to Lune in the sway of bodies, and Lune held her hands in a fist, ready to curse anyone that would let her mother die. The red haired woman hovered over Lune's mother like she was a kite, blowing the air, willing her to live. Lune's mother had full round breasts buried under the daffodil dress, and her hair was matted to her mouth like clods of dirt. Lune thought she could see insects fly from her mother's mouth and ears, when her father appeared and knelt beside her mother and the paramedics. The paramedic's hands were shaking on Marcrina's face when Marcrina began to cough up water, the baby pool tipped over and made a bigger pool in the grass, barely touching Lune's toes again, the tight leather straps of her sandals burning her ankles. She clawed at her own ankles, pulling the sandals off her feet.

Lune thought that her mother had been dead and had been revived because her father had returned to them. There was a tourniquet wrapped around Marcrina's arm and a stethoscope placed at the rise and fall of her breast. Lune thought that her mother's dying would make her skin turn blue, but it remained as brown as ever, and the daffodil of her dress lay shaking on her hips and her breasts. The paramedics tried to make Lune's mother go to the hospital, but her father wouldn't let them take her. He undressed her in the warm glow of the bathroom, the light of the ceiling, making new daffodils on her body. Lune saw her father put her mother in the bath water, saw him pull her hair away from her face, her shoulder blades shuddered at the touch of the water. Lune could hear them whispering to each other and those whispers became the things that flew out of her mother's mouth like insects. She tried to make out the lines of the wings and the plump black segments of their bodies, but the insects were hazy and only the buzz of letters could be recognized. No full words. Just moving mouths and shoulder blades and the slow crashing of bathtub water.

After he helped put her mother to bed, Lune's

father heat up cold cocido in a pot and they ate together in their kitchen nook. Lune's father put his wife's insects in his mouth and ate them. He ate the secrets and Lune and her father ate the soup together, and they were happy that she wasn't dead.

# SANTA MUERTE AND THE POCHA BRIGADE

THERE WERE three hospitals in Cenote City, but the Santa Muerte Hospital was the one that was most alive. From the window in Dr. de la O's office, the statue of Santa Muerte seemed to be floating above the hospital garden, but she knew better than that. She was real, porcelain mist and black paint speckled with stars. Her arms were outstretched as if to cradle her, and the dark gapes on her bony wrists were the entrance wounds that the spirits of the dead would enter through, seeking some kind of solace, but no judgment, for they knew better than that. Santa Muerte never judges. She only listens.

When the statue of Santa Muerte was first erected in the garden, her feet were bolted to the ground, but then they became unhinged and so she was hung and swung on thick wire cords like a pendulum. A gate was placed around her so that visitors wouldn't get too close to the statue, lest they be dismembered or beheaded. Every Friday, the gardeners came and pruned the roses bushes around Santa Muerte and then they would set off sprinklers that showered the garden with a pink mist.

"Why is the water pink?" de la O asked the gardeners one day.

"Because that's her favorite color," they said.

"No, it's not."

"It's *her* favorite color. This Muerte."

96

After that, de la O bought Santa Muerte pink candles once a week and set them at her feet. The candles were like tiny mouths opening wide in an O, like her name, moaning for Santa Muerte to listen.

The Pocha Brigade appeared the week before the hospital was shut down. The three teenage girls all wore black denim moto vests with lacy pink bras underneath and high waisted black parachute pants that looked like balloons from de la O's window. They each carried a pink plastic Jack O' Lantern pail in the hook of their arms and one of the girls, who appeared to be the leader, knelt below Santa Muerte and began to light a smudge stick, making a halo of smoke around her head. Another girl tore the stick from her hand, relit the tip and passed the smoke from her toes to her head and did the same to the remaining three girls. The vests had the words, Pocha Brigade on the back in hot pink old English letters. de la O realized that one of the young women was her niece. She hadn't seen her since she was a little girl, but she knew it was her.. Dark green eyes and wavy brown hair frizzed around her face like a spiders' web. Her niece looked up and waved at her from the bottom. She waved back and he thought, *How could she possibly know that it's me? How can she make out my face? How can I make out her face now?*

de la O took the elevator down to the hospital garden, it's ding making the young women jump up in fright, but her niece stood there in the mist, waving the smudge stick, which smelled to her like burnt sugar in a pan. The rose bushes bent their backs and touched their toes, ballerina-style as she walked past.

She pushed them away, their leaves scraping his hands, but the thorns were kind and didn't prick her. She called out her niece's name, *Yoli*, and as she did, she realized that she had never said her name before, and she felt a sort of shame in doing so now, the pink mist on her arms making her feel warm and shiver.

Yoli tossed the smudge stick in her pail and walked over to her, her face trying to find a note of recognition. de la O was surprised when she put her hand out so she could shake it. The three other women pulled their moto vests closed and picked up their pails, their hands shaking in their handles.

"This is my Tia," Yoli laughed nervously, lighting a skinny cigarette wrapped in polk-dotted paper.

"Don't smoke in a hospital, Yoli!" One of the other girls shouted.

de la O tried to ask Yoli about her mother, but she wanted to talk about Santa Muerte instead. A hot wind began to blow on their bodies. The sun was setting, and de la O began to look for the pink promised moon. She always tried to take photos of strawberry moons on her phone but they always appeared as blurry red specks in the lens. The night lights in the garden would be switched on soon.

"We wanted to come and see her," Yoli said. "One last time. What do you think they'll do with her?"

"Who?" de la O asked.

"You know who. They have their eyes on you. They have their eyes on this place. My senses tell me."

# W E'RE ANIMALS DROWNING

CENOTE WATER and my mother's tears were creeping into the zoo. The monkeys had begun to shudder slowly in their cages, and the lion had woken up from its nap, the water touching the tip of its claws like a prayer. Me and Nico walked around the zoo in circles, picking up popcorn wrappers and maps smudged with dirt and baby finger prints and cherry punch smiles. As we walked up the stairs to the elephant habitat, the water swayed past us like a serpent. I touched my finger to the water and tasted it. I knew it was my mother's tears and I could see that my son knew it too.

Nico asked for bus fare so that he could go home and I gave him an extra five dollars, so he could get lunch on the way. The sun was bright, which meant that it was getting to be later in the afternoon, but there were still mothers pushing their babies in strollers, pointing at the animals that stared back at them, their eyes asking about the water they knew nothing about. I had been one of those mothers a long time ago. When Nico was small, I took him all around the city on the bus, buying Chinese to-go plates from the Tower District and sitting cross-legged at the parks lake, spooning rice into his little mouth.

On my pay days , I took Nico to the carnival in the park. The Concrete Carnival is a large strip with a roller coaster and carousel and Ferris Wheel looming over mechanical lady bugs and helicopters. One sunny afternoon, as we were riding the train, I looked over the railing and saw a dog had drowned in the lake, a black fur patch in the water. I felt a cool breeze rustle in the leaves, and I covered Nico's eyes with my own hands, but he pushed them away, and we saw many patches of fur in the water, floating, and I tried to cover his eyes one more time, the train shaking its way into the mouth of a tunnel.

# NICO IN THE PUMPKIN FLOWERS

THE FLOWERS GREW at the edge of the Belmont cemetery and Nico tugged at them under the new moon. Even though it was dark, he knew the exact green hue of the leaves because his mother had been bringing him to those pumpkin flowers ever since he was a boy. He only found four flowers sprouting out of the ground and he named them *almost flowers*. Like the *almost sky* and the *almost night*. He thought of his grandmother's dark skin, the lines around her brown eyes, the ring of bleach in her hair because she wanted to look like she lived in Old Hollywood and drank tequila at bars with rich brown men draping her shoulder blades in rubies and pearls. He had seen her bury many things in the ground as well.

He took the four flowers and put them in the small black satchel that his grandmother had given him when he was a little boy. She had scolded him when he said that it was for girls because it was soft and shaped like an oyster's shell. He had taken the bag and shoved it in his dresser drawer, a sort of garbage shoot where he sent things that he didn't have the heart for. Amongst fingerless gloves and cheap comic books and strips of black-and-white photos of himself and his mother, the black satchel sat until that night, when he decided that he would go to the pumpkin flowers. He thought he could see his grandmother watching him from her kitchen window, the lace from her curtains like an eye that would open and shut on him, her dyed blonde hair blowing from the old electrical fan on her table-top, the whir of the little fan blades like a beating heart. She mouthed his name, the way she did when he was born. He was standing at another burial for his mother. The satchel devoid of color, a hole in his hand, protection for his almost mother, la Lune.

# $\mathcal{T}$OURNIQUET BABY

JONNY SET up a clinic outside of Piper's Pizza, which was convenient for Stevie because he had the early shift at work. He had begun to have chronic pain in his left eye socket and had begun to forget how to sing the words in the mariachi songs. Jonny flashed a green light in his eyeball and looked in it like it was the night.

"What kind of Jay Gatsby bullshit is this, Jonny? Green light?"

Jonny laughed and pulled a tube of pills out of the cabinet. The little bus rattled as the door opened. Lune was wearing her hair in a slick black ponytail with a bumper bang swooped on one side. Jonny smiled at her and then shoved a large orange pill into Stevie's mouth.

"Take these every eight hours. But better yet, stop thinking about your teacher. He's like poison in your head."

"And you already know it's cliché to be in love with your teacher," Lune laughed, her hand in the candy jar. She pulled out a blue stick of rock candy and ran it over her mouth like lipstick.

Professor Mundo had never sent a reply to his text message, but he had spoken to him during his last clown class. Stevie had arrived late and sat in the very back, rows and rows of easels in front of his own, a slash of paint to hide his pain. Professor Mundo was talking more than he usually did. He usually let them paint quietly on their own when the models were there, but words were coming out of his mouth and floating around the rooms like bubbles. The model had her back arched and she looked like a tree at the cenote, her long curly brown hair like roots, the veins of her hand shaking in the roots, her elbow trying to steady itself on her kneecap. Just as Stevie was making the dip of her chin, he felt Dr. Mundo walk behind him. The model switched sides and pulled the hair away from her face. Professor. Mundo's feet paused and walked on. Stevies's eyes caught on the model's eyes and he felt a dull ache in his spine. Her eyes were blood-shot, like pink flowers blooming on brown paint.

Professor Mundo pulled up a stool and sat next to Stevie and Stevie hoped that he wouldn't see the shaking in his hand. Steven began to paint the model's pink flower eyeballs. Professor Mundo smelled like lemon grass and leather, which surprised Stevie, who had always imagined that Professor Mundo would smell either like an ocean tide or a cactus, one of those extremes.

"Steven, I got your text message. I'm sorry, I couldn't reply. I'm not allowed to date my pupils." Steven began to apologize profusely, but Professor Mundo said that he didn't need to be sorry for anything.

"How did you do it, Steven. How did you make that boy disappear at the cenote?" He was whispering. "That boy was gone for hours."

Stevie replied with a red ribbon of paint on the

woman's hair, then he said, "I couldn't tell you how I did it. I don't even know where the boy went during those hours. I don't know what happened."

Professor Mundo reached over him and dabbed his fingers in blue paint and touched it to the woman's eyes.

"If you can make people disappear like that, then The Generales will be scared of you and they'll be scared of your friends. Clowns and magic will be in danger here."

The blue on the canvas looked like veins from the eyes and they began to trickle and bleed and trickle and bleed.

# CLOWN BEAST AND LOVING

LUNE AND JONNY decided that they would go to the Concrete Carnival for their first date. Jonny put a black letter jacket over his pale green scrub pants, his pack of cigarettes sticking out of his pocket like a smile. The package said "Xquic Cigarettes" and it made her think of Nico's father because he used to smoke that brand, and she wondered where Nico's father was at that very moment, and she hoped that he was safe in Xibalba. Jonny drove them to the park in his little white car that looked like a rolly poly insect with antennas. His head almost hit the roof because he was a tall man, but the car still fit him in some strange way, and Lune noticed that his eyes slanted every time he hit a stoplight. She also noticed that he was wearing new glasses that looked like they were expensive. She had never seen glasses like that before.

Lune watched his foot every time it hit the gas and she found herself wanting to know what kind of cartoons he watched when he was a baby and if he had ever gone fishing with his father at the cenote. Since he was a few years younger than she was, she figured that he must have gone to the cenote long after she did, and that there must have been a ghost of her own father and a ghost of herself standing at the mouth of the cenote, arguing about what was really in the water. She imagined Jonny as a young brown boy, laughing as he did now, holding his father now, not becoming a complete de la O, but more like a current of water that his father let flow from the palm of his hand. Jonny was another thing altogether and Lune liked all the lines of his body and the way those lines set themselves on the outline of the park. The city was a jumble of shapes behind the chain link fence of the carnival. That city she saw then was made up of old buildings and abandoned churches and a hospital garden.

Lune could feel the hunger in her stomach. She had gone nearly half a day without eating, but she felt her hand claw at Jonny's when they stopped in front of the lion's mouth. She had enough energy for that. The statue of the lion had a water fountain inside of its mouth, it's tongue a loose grip from a roar. The silence of the clown beast was whirring in the dead breeze of the park. Jonny took his phone out from his pocket and began snapping pictures down the lion's mouth and the lion looked like it would swallow him whole. Lune wondered what would happen if the lion did swallow him. She wondered if his father would mourn his son. She wondered if the lions would spit out his blood and if it would turn to a nighttime mist of fireflies, a thing she had never seen before, but had always hoped for. She stepped on Jonny's blue shoe and took his hand, which he gripped back, and it felt warm and shaking. "My father is dead," Jonny told her. "He died when I was a kid."

Lune was surprised at what Jonny said and she was surprised that Jonny was wearing a thick black letterman jacket in the summertime. Cenote City summers were always hot, and the way the heat spat from the sky always depended on which mouth of the city you were standing under. Jonny's mouth was cold because he had just drank the water from the fountain. Lune took his mouth and the slant of his eyes at the same time, and it felt like the doom of the moon. She could smell the pomade in his hair, the way it slicked past his ear lobe reminded her of the first time she saw him in the arcade at the pizza parlor. He had looked at her nervously then, and there was only a half rhythm to his shaking then because they didn't know each other. His shaking was at full capacity there at the water fountain, and she felt herself crush against him, taking him in, the J on his jacket a quick swirl, the end of an afternoon.

Lune pushed Jonny away and walked towards the dragon roller coaster, the dragon's mouth in a tight grip on the track. She remembered riding it when she was little girl, how the car rattled against her back and how she was afraid that it would snap the bones in her back and that her bones would turn into beads and then into dust. Jonny walked over to her and put his hand on the iron gate that enclosed the roller coaster and she could feel him staring at her face, the green from his scrubs fading away in the encroaching shade from the trees. He pulled her close and kissed her face, and she kept her eyes on the dragon on her tracks. She could see her mother's tears and the cenote water running along the periphery of the carnival, and could hear the slow rush of them draining into the sewer below.

Jonny's pomade was against her face and she took

his mouth again, but this time she only gave him half of her, like a half smile, but she let him put his hand under her dress and between her legs and run circles under there, slow circles and his shaking, which was the first thing that brought him to her in the first place. The statue animals in the Concrete Carnival had simmered their voices and the living zoo animals were like drum beats in their cages, slowing to sleep in their dens, the promise of the half-moon, a lullaby, a promise that their death would come one day, but not that summer night.

Lune knew that Jonny had volunteered at the clinics because he had the capacity for goodness and he was hers that afternoon and his shaking was equal to his joy. She could see the tiny houses of Storylandia in the distance, brick reds and blue hues and paper lanterns that dotted trees like charms from her mother's necklace. The charms her mother held tight in her hands for solace, when the sky felt pink and dying. The air felt warm to Lune now and Jonny's jacket was appearing again, becoming too much of a thing, growing on his bones, and the cars on the highway reached their full hum because it was night and the two blessed each other under the moon.

# BEAUTIFY AND HIDE

MY MOTHER THOUGHT I should cut my hair, so that The Generales wouldn't recognize me. So that it would be easier for us all to escape. Knowing Carlo made that an easy thing to take care of. For the longest time, we used to joke around and say that we weren't just friends, just acquaintances, but the water spilling from the cenote snuffed that joke out like vapor. Carlo lost his beauty license when he went to visit his grandmother in Colorado for three months and forgot to update his paperwork. He refused to pay for a new license, and instead, decided to do hair in his apartment, which was a hole in the ground. Not a hole in the wall. That would be cliché and Carlo could never stand clichés. His apartment was exactly six steps deep in a complex across the street from the fairgrounds, the roof of it sticking out from trees and bushes like a little angry hat. We all thought that this was a fitting place for Carlo to live.

No one ever had to knock on the door at La Lab because the little door was always unlocked. Still I knocked on the door on a Saturday and I waited. Yoli opened the door in a pink bonnet, snapping a picture of me on her phone.

"This is for the "Before" picture," she said. "The one that goes on the wall."

"How did you know I was coming?" I asked and then I remembered that Jonny and Yoli were cousins and he must have told her, and I was mad at myself for forgetting something so important.

Carlo stood behind a Mexican woman with bright red hair, teasing her hair with a rat tail comb. To me she looked like she was fifty-five, and I wondered what it would be like if she and my mother ever crossed paths. The woman was holding tarots cards and fanning herself like she was Marie Antoinette.

"These fumes always get to me so hot, baby. You really need some fans in here." She said.

"I'm sorry, Mrs. Soliz," he said, standing her up and walking her over to a green latticed mirror hanging on the wall. "I'm sorry. I hope you think it's worth it."

Mrs. Soliz began to giggle behind her fan and her breasts looked like perfect planets under her polka-dotted poncho dress.

"Mrs. Soliz, have you ever noticed that you always cover your mouth when you smile?" Carlo asked her.

Yoli laughed from the corner of the room, like she was a rose blooming in the fumes, playing with the knob on the TV set with one hand, a shot of vodka in the other hand.

"Don't you all love Mrs. Soliz's dress?" Yoli asked and we said, yes. I would have said yes even if Yoli hadn't made it. The dress was beautiful on that woman. It made me think of a book I had read once that talked about beauty and the sublime. That certain things were beautiful because they make us think of death.

I sat on the seat below the hairdryer and began to play with the ends of my hair. I imagined each strand

111

of my brown hair threaded into sewing needles. Mrs. Soliz tucked a wad of cash into Marco's crisp white collared shirt and she became like a passing cloud in that sky, floating out of La Lab and its illegal fumes. Carlo took a rag to the swivel chair and wiped away the last trace of Mrs. Soliz's hair. It looked like fire fell from that rag because the room was growing dim and the sun outside the window was going down fast.

When I sat in swivel chair, I began to think about how I cut my hair the first time Nico's father made me cry, how I cut my hair again the day they slid his body into a cold crypt, pushing him into the wall like a dresser drawer. I cut my hair even though I knew he would never see me again. Kahlo cut her hair when Rivera fucked her sister and cut her body and her heart in two. I felt a shiver when Carlo tapped his hand on my shoulder blade, his palm out, his hand like a blade.

"You want me to cut it to here?" he asked.

"No."

He tapped his palm in the middle of my neck.

"Here?" he asked.

"No," I said.

I took my own palm and held it to my own face, to where my mouth was.

"Here," I said.

As Carlo cut my hair, I began to read the poem that was written on the wall and thought of the story that I had been told about that poem.

The story goes that a poeta used to live in the apartment before Carlo lived there, and she was the one who wrote it. One afternoon, she began to write the poem in a brown calligraphy pen in big swirly letters, and when all the neighbors in the apartment complex saw that she was writing the poem, they were happy because they loved her words. They would stay up at night reading them from tiny paper books that she made with her own hands and the poems began to feel like they were taking root and sprouting in their own hands as they read them.

One night, the poeta disappeared and no one could bear to paint over the poem on the wall. So there it was and will always be, on the wall of Marco's kitchen. The poem brought him solace when he couldn't sleep at night or when he felt like he didn't want to cut hair anymore. He wanted all the women in Cenote City to walk in there and drink from that poem that was like trees and vapor and shade and blood and jewels on the wall.

CARLO CUT my hair to look like a little triangle. By the time I was looking at myself in the mirror the night had fallen completely from the trees, and Yoli was humming and stitching a blanket. I had never seen her make anything like a blanket, only dresses and suits and dolls with half moon slits for eyes. I wondered who the blanket was for because it didn't look like it was for a baby and it didn't look like it was for a woman.

"A shroud," she told me. She held the fabric over her head and the old electric fan made it balloon blue in the air. "A shroud," she told me. *A shroud.*

"For who?" I asked.

"I don't know yet," she said. Her shadow humming her song from the corner of the room and the beauty salon fumes were like flowers in my lungs and my eyes and then there was a knock at the door. Yoli went to look through the peep hole in the door. She began to whisper. It was The Generales. It was their men looking for me. Men in white tailored suits and pulsing flesh, like a breathing cloudy splotch in the night. Men with booming voices and sweaty necks and blue eyes like Cortez. We told Carlo to open the door because we knew that was the safest thing to do. I stood behind the kitchen wall and read the poem from the beautiful woman again. I could hear tree leaves rustle outside and the smoke from Yuri's lit cigarette was a necklace that I wanted to choke myself with. The smoke smelled like a ripe peach and I thought of the skin of it burning bright like the sun that had fallen just minutes before. The skin of the peach was ripped and slashed and the juice of it made smoke to appease one woman's mouth and to calm another woman, shaking in a kitchen. I wanted to make that fruit a song, a hex for the pale goblins planted at the door, asking for me. It wasn't enough that The Generales had claimed my mother. They wanted me too, her flesh song and when Carlo had turned them away and shut the door, cenote water began to stream under the door and touched at my ankles to remind me that I was still in the kitchen, waiting to be found.

# PENDULUM

WHEN MARCRINA BEGINS TO CRY, it feels like razor blades knocking around inside her skull. She never knew where her tear ducts were, until she had begun to have her crying jags. Her tears feel like tiny needles pulling thread through her tear ducts and the soft pink of her skin tissue. She thinks about these colors in the rim of her eye, how they flame bright pink, but when she cries, the rims of her eyes feel tender like honeycomb tripe that has been stewed in a hot pot for hours and hours.

When Marcrina begins to cry, the cenote looks like a giant eyeball, a blue that she never knew about before the hospitals closed, before she began to pull babies out of their mothers, brown babies, pale faced and new. It was death that made her see this kind of blue. In the eyeball she sees the clouds of the water and thinks that they're like the clods of dirt that boys threw at her when she was young. When she is bent over the wide mouth of the cenote, her head feels like a pendulum on her shoulder, heavy and light at the same time and her hair swings to the left and the right, and the blonde hair knots when it becomes wet with her tears and dirt and sweat and the sweet perfume that dapples her skin. The tears make the perfume feel like poison on her skin.

When Marcrina cries, she begins to smell the skin of all the dead babies she delivered. She wants to fly and find the tiny holes where each and every one of them reside in the dirt, but she cannot fly when she's at the mouth of the cenote and crying into it. She has married herself to the cenote. She wants to find the tiny holes and the tiny coffins that each baby is buried in and she wants to polish the dirt from their nails shaped like tiny rectangles. She wants to run her fingertips over the lids of their eyes. She wants to ask them for permission to make her own eyes shut, so she won't cry anymore, but they cannot give her their blessing because they don't have the capacity to give or to love her in return.

# ALTAR BOY

WHEN MY MOTHER WAS A GIRL, she fell in love with an altar boy at Santa Muerte Hospital. She wasn't much older than Nico is now. I've seen pictures of her, the way she looked back then. Dark hair and dark slanted eyes. She would walk past the hospital every day on her way home from school, and the hospital began to call out to her from its windows like hundreds of eyes and mouths. She would walk the hallways and listen to the tiny muted voices, and she would walk around the hospital garden and she would nap in the leaves, until she would hear the gardeners coming with their rakes and brooms and plastic bags and she would steal away from the garden gate before they would ever see her, pulling white flowers from trees and crushing them against her thighs before she went to bed.

And then she fell in love with the altar boy. Inside the hospital walls, on the third floor, at the end of the hallway, there was a door, and when she opened that door, she found a large church with rows and rows of pews plastered with fliers that advertised rooms for rent in the Tower District and delicatessens and needle drives and cheap champagne breakfasts at Storylandia. The altar boy believed himself a priest and was there teaching his lessons, a buzz of children around him. They listened to him for a time and then quickly faded in and out of the distance, their feet pounding the stone floor and their brown fingers tracing the stained glass of the window, pictures of trees impregnating the open hands of Blood Moon and her much honored sons, One Hanuhpu and Xbalanque. The children began to give way to their longing, running through the corridors of the church, drinking wine in the kitchen, crushing dandelions in their hair, and laughing at the way the sunlight passed through the church in new hues of their own design.

So my mother began to come to the hospital church every night, and watched the altar boy light candles and pray, his face like pale bleached bone in the light, and his black glasses marking the geometry of his face. She wanted to smoke the cool of his brain and find herself there.

One day, one of the altar boy's pupils came to her and took her wrist in a gentle way and whispered to my mother.

"His favorite color in the world is red, like a demon," the tiny pupil said.

So she began to dress herself in red dresses and red patent leather shoes and painted her lips red from a pot and painted her fingertips with red polish with fat specks of red glitter. She sat in the far corner of the church, even though she hated everything about going to Mass, except for the smell of incense cones and prayer paper. My mother's family had stopped going to church long ago and the only saint she ever wanted to pray to was her Holy Death.

She watched the altar boy rebuke other children when they didn't recite their prayers in the proper manner and she watched him read from his book to the children near the stained glass tree. If the other children forgot their prayer books, he turned them away and he called it righteous anger.

My mother waited and waited for him in the dark of the church, until one day he spoke to her, and she spoke to him back. She had willed it so, for every night when she went to bed, she spun in circles and crushed his name with smoke to her eyes and her throat in a song she had heard once at the Concrete Carnival.

After they spoke, the altar boy shaved his head and the remnants of black stemmed hair fell beneath his head, but all the prayers lay hooked on his tongue, slow shivering and quiet. The altar boy sat beside her in the church and shaking, let her put her mouth on his, and then he kissed her back and touched her and he became something else to her. The altar boy was like the stained glass windows, colored in fragments, lines between bones and blood, the glow of the burning sun to the face, a scar to the pale webbing of his hands. And after the boy kissed her, she saw the shame in his eyes, and she watched him run and run and run through the halls of the church, passing like insects into candle wax, his body robed in black and meter, and even though she knew her body was greater than his, she mourned for the illusion that she had created for herself.

She began to undo the love she felt for the altar boy and cool the warm blood she felt at the neon flicker of the church emptied of children. She wrote his name with crayon on prayer paper and stuck it to the red hues of cherry gum that came from her mouth. She plucked petals from the hospital garden and buried colored stones in the ground like they were her own mother's bones. She found her mother's sewing needles and coaxed the dirt out of her fingernails because her love for the altar boy resided even there.

And when my mother told me about this altar boy, I knew that she was still undoing her love, the touch of him tapping on the blonde covered skull of her woman's body, the slow pulse of him encased in every third teardrop that spliced through her own dark eyes in the moon of light, a limpia forever, the salty tears of orifices tattooed in red ink with holy verses that she was unable to whisper and unwilling to understand, the slow buzz of a TV set, a cold throat of tequila blown on the altar boy's bones like smoke.

# YOU DON'T WITCH RITE

JONNY SAYS he knows a witch named Miranda who can make my mother's eyes shut. When he first told me this, I wanted to slap him in the face, even though his face is always rough and beautiful. Then I realized that he was talking about witching, about magic, that he wasn't speaking literally and then I felt bad for making him feel pained by me, however little it may be.

As I lay in his bed, I wondered why men never have top sheets on their bed, how they can be incapable of this kind of loving, of this kind of domesticity. His bottom sheet is bright blue like the cenote at night, his bed, my forest that is crowded with trees and is unending for me. He likes to play the stereo when we have sex in his room. And he smells different than other men. He's hands are scrubbed clean with alcohol and cotton balls and his hands are soft and shaking and warm to the touch. He sets a mirror next to the bed *to catch the afternoon*, he says and when he explains it this way. I know that he never says anything without intentionality. He brushes my hair as I lay on my back and then he kisses my face in the dark.

I ask him to tell me more about this witch named Miranda. I ask him where she lives. When I first start asking him this, all he tells me is that she lives on the north side of the valley in a house surrounded by a doll buggy garden and Chocolate Cosmos and trees. I ask him, *what kind of doll buggies are they?* He tells me they are antique doll buggies bought at auctions, the highest bidder always a woman with a black lace glove with the fingers cut off, a woman named Miranda who lives with her daughter and her daughter's lover and their twin daughters. I ask Jonny if the witch's house is beautiful. He tells me that it's not beautiful, but it sits at the mouth of an invisible sea and it is because of that sea that the witch can cure my mother of what ails her. *The witch is waiting for your mother, so that they can walk off into the invisible sea together. She knows it.* He kisses me hard on the mouth when he says this, the warm crush of his skin tells me. He traces the shape of a flute on my shoulder bone. He tells me, *the witch is waiting for your mother and maybe she's waiting for you, too.*

# EL PAYASO

THE DAY after the divers disturbed the cenote, a car of clowns came to rescue my mother from Cenote City. And even though I knew she wouldn't want to go with them, I wanted to hear them out. I knew that they could help my mother get out of here fast. They weren't the kind of clowns that Stevie wants to be, Clowns of Everything. They are classic clowns, they are acrobats, they are painted faces for a price. As in many fantastical stories, the clowns came in three. They were brown clowns from the south side of the valley, stocky in build with thick muscular necks and blue veins pumping blood like ropes beneath their skin.

The funny thing was that only one of them went by "El Payaso." They were like me and my friends and Nico. They couldn't speak Spanish either. I was surprised when my mother actually invited them inside her house. I saw her kitchen curtains shake a little when they sat at her table. The only man the house is accustomed to is Nico and I think it's always accepted him not because he's blood, but because he's loving. The name of the other clowns have slipped my mind, but one wore green and the other was wearing a red leather vest with polka dots and cowboy boots that he tapped on the wooden floors, which made my bones feel like they were fluttering around inside my body. I could tell that this cowboy clown was handsome under his make-up because of the shape of his eyes and the sharpness of his jaws. He looked like he could have dug out the entire cenote with his muscular arms, but the slight ticks in his face made me not want to love him. I could tell that he belonged to another because he was squirming the entire time and checking his watch.

El Payaso said they had begun to hear rumors about the cenote spilling over, that divers had come, that their trespassing was making the blue waters levitate and scatter like the leaves. They wanted to help my mother escape and be safe. It would be advantageous for everyone involved. *She'd be the star in our circus show.* They'd have a place for her to drain her eyes and they would pay her money and she could send money to me. She could send money to her grandson.

El Payaso jumped with a start when he saw Nico staring at us through the kitchen window. Nico's hair fell across one of his eyes and his laugh was like a rooster crow.

"Are those clowns?" Nico asked.

The three clowns looked at Nico like they wanted to smash his skull in, and I clutched at the knife in my pocket. Nico's smile turned to a straight line on his face, like the flat sunshine skies he used to draw on brown paper bags when he was a baby. The cenote looked like a wide blue mouth in the distance, a gash in the earth trying to take my mother away from me, trying to take a grandmother from the boy in the window. Nico kept his eyes on the clowns. Two brown eyes unstitching six brown eyes.

I handed a lemon and a knife and a cutting board to the cowboy clown.

"I stopped cutting things for men a long time ago," I told him.

He looked at me and grinned and reached over and thumbed the veins in my wrist.

"I can see blue in there," he told me.

"Will there be someone to watch my mother when she sleeps during the day? She needs lots of rest. She wouldn't want someone actually watching her. Maybe someone outside her door?"

El Payaso began to slice into the bright yellow lemon skin and the other two clowns looked at each other for the answers to my question.

"We pretty much sleep out of our suitcases," El Payaso said. "We stay at motels. Your mother would always have her own room. We have a pretty good team of boys that watch over us. One crew to watch us sleep during the day and another crew that watches us all night during the show."

"How many nights will you be here?" Nico asked from outside the kitchen window. Smoke rose from underneath the window. Another serpent. The soup on the stove simmered on the pot, and I ladled out three ox-tails into three bowls and flooded them with broth and carrots and corn, and I could taste the blood broth of the soup without even putting it in my mouth, and I wondered why white sage always smells like rotting meat to me. I saw Nico walking towards the cenote with his blue burning bowl, the smoke sprouting out of his hand happily. I set the three soup bowls before the clowns and just as they were going to dip their spoons in the soup, my mother bloomed in the doorway and spoke.

"Take us to your circus show. Take us to the fairgrounds. You're here for just one night. I want to see what this is all about. I have a say in the matter."

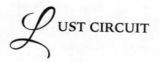

# LUST CIRCUIT

THE INSIDE of the circus tent was draped all in red like tongues lapping at the day. The daylight, a slash at the top of the tent, was disappearing into the clouds, and I could still smell my mother's perfume even though she was far away from me. The clowns had offered us a box close to the ring, but Nico refused to sit there because he didn't want to be under the bright lights. My mother went to sit in the box by herself. She was dressed in a green dress that shimmered in the lights, a garden of ruffles and tulle around her neck, her lips like a rosebud on her face.

"What the hell are we doing here? Grandma's gonna start to cry soon. She should be getting her rest."

Nico had slicked his hair back with pomade and was wearing a blue shirt with black polka dots that he had bought years ago at a thrift store. He had been waiting for the day it would fit him. He ate popcorn from a red and white paper sack with the words *El Payaso !presente!* in fat black letters. He put his hand on my knee and asked me to stop shaking my leg. That shaking was something that I was glad that he hadn't inherited. And even though his eyes always looked like mine, they were in a different kind of slant that afternoon, and when the lights dimmed and the music started, his voice began to tremor and then fade back into his throat. I sat closer to him as more people packed the bleachers. He smelled like sage, and I wondered if anyone else could smell it on him too.

A see-saw appeared in the tent sky and Payaso was on top of it, his feet looking delicate on the plank of wood. He crossed himself, the trinity leaving tiny fingerprints that glowed red on his forehead and shoulder cap. Payaso tipped his hat to my mother and scanned the crowd, his feet on the board like it was a wave, bobbing with fish and water. A tiny orchestra played in the ring of dirt that was below. There was a violin that sounded like a wail and then I saw that El Payaso had pulled his sunglasses off of his face and was looking into the crowd. I began to feel the heads of the audience turn and turn and turn and it seemed then that each and every face was looking at me, and El Payaso was looking at me, his mouth hard, and I knew his skin was scorched brown, not by the sunshine, but by the hot lights of this place and I knew that my mother's body could be safe there, under that tent, if I would only let her go.

There were loud shots and smoke, and we stood there waiting for El Payaso to jump, but instead Nico pushed me off of my seat and onto the bleachers, the hot sting of metal on my knees. The audience was becoming undone and I knew The Generales wouldn't let my mother go. I felt my son's arms pushing on my back and I could hear his voice and breath on my neck and the violin had stopped playing, and he was screaming for Macrina. I saw my mother's green dress floating like a balloon in that crush of smoke, the large circus tent billowing like a red cloud in the black expanse.

Nico and I were rushing against gravel and bodies, my shoes filling with rocks. All the clowns were running to their trucks in a flurry of reds and yellows and greens. The last time I saw El Payaso, he was pulling a donkey into a trailer and the animal's eyes were wild. There would be no refuge in this circus after all. Nico tripped and fell on a knot of electrical cords. He cried out when my mother pulled him up by his wrists, her green dress still flying the dust. We took hands amongst the crowds of people rushing away and we ran, cars whirring by, through the old beat of our streets.

# THE POISON PARTY

THE CENOTE WATER was running through the city fast, but it was still Nico's birthday. He was turning fifteen. Marcrina planned a party to begin early in the afternoon, before she started crying and the tourists came. She had dinosaur plates for Nico since it was his birthday, but Nico insisted that they use her pink dishes because they were her favorite and she rarely had an occasion to have a party. The sun was bright and hot, splattered through the canopy that shaded the birthday table that we sat at near the cenote.

Jonny arrived with a blue cake that had a combustion of star confetti and green frosting. Marcrina had made a strawberry pie because Nico preferred it to cake and he began to cut into it before they even began the main course. For years, Marcrina had forgotten about Jonny Ex Oh from the hospital garden, but there he was again, sitting at her table, now a grown man, but his face still looked the same. Slanted eyes, black swoop of hair over the eye. The cenote streamed still around Jonny, but the ducklings from the pond stirred around his feet in a circle of white frothy feathers and webbed feet like orange splashes of paint in the dirt.

"My mom would like to come and visit you Marcrina," Jonny said, scooping black chile out of a pot with a silver spoon with a spike at the end.

My mother's mother and grandmother and great-grandmother had used the spoon, and she hopes to give it to me one day. She knows I don't like to cook, but she says that I can use the spiky end of the spoon when I walk alone in the dark.

Nico was sitting at the cenote and dumping plastic flowers out of vases. He had parted his hair severely, and I could see the smooth line that ran across his head and the swirl of hair in the back of his head like a button. When he was small, my mother used to touch her finger to that very spot and say, *grandson, this little circle means you're mischievous. All the little boys like you have this.* Nico was melting plastic flowers into glass, the colors melding into reds and greens and yellows, the smell of burning plastic poring its way through the air like bees.

"What are you going to do with those, Nico?" My mother asked.

"I'm going to sprinkle the tops with glitter and sell them to the tourists when they get here. Maybe I'll write Cenote City on the bottle."

"The tourists will buy anything you put out here. I could turn my pockets inside out and get them to buy the things that fall out. They want to come here and get something quick. They just come here to party," my mother told Jonny.

"So, when is your mother going to come and see me? We used to be close, you know." My mother was smiling at Jonny, even though she had tried to keep a tight face, not because she didn't want to smile but because she wanted to save her energy for that evening. She didn't think she would find time for a nap before her crying jags began.

~

I COULD TELL that my mother liked my outfit. I was wearing skintight black jeans that striped my legs like wet paint. My hair was still freshly cut by Carlo, a smooth black triangle of hair that made me look like I was regal sitting next to Jonny. I can tell my mother thinks me and Jonny are a beautiful thing, by the way she nods her head when Jonny talks.

"And where is your mother now, Jonny? Is she in LA?" My mother asked.

"She's not there. She's not in the valley either."

"Then where is she?"

My mother picked up her teacup and took a drink. I could tell the tea was already cold and she watched Nico drink quickly from his own pink cup, slurping, tea falling from his face in green and golden drips. In green and golden drips, he began to choke and fall out of his chair, shaking like his bones were made of glass and they were breaking. I began to scream and pull at his body, dirt flying under his shoes, his body bent over my arms like a crescent. Jonny stuck his fingers inside Nico's mouth and pulled a flower out, the eye of the flower filled with tiny seeds that moved and there were many little insects like pin pricks. Jonny's fingers were bruised and shaking and there was a veil of dust on his face. A trail of birds skimmed across the opening of the cenote, circling to the tune of Marcrina's wind chime, slowly falling sideways, the chime that hung from her pink house like jewels on a neck.

# Mito

Jonny and his mother know how to get past the mountains. They said that if we want to go on living, we have to find a way to leave Cenote City. We have all seen the mountains before. They look like giants that have been slaughtered and covered with blankets, patches of grass and dirt and knots and vines. Jonny's mother puts money in a hole in the ground, the old Mexican way. She takes twenty dollars into the bank and exchanges them for one hundred dollar bills, so that she can stack the bills neatly in the dirt like bodies, a card stack of bones and flesh, one on top of the other. She has been doing this all so that she can save her friends.

# NECROMANCY FOR NICO

EVEN THOUGH THE cenote was beginning to spill over, people still came for the night show. Yoli was praying at the water's edge in a dress speckled with glow-in-the-dark green eyeballs that rolled every time they heard someone say something stupid. Dr. Mundo was on the north side of the cenote painting on the canvas that sat on top a large easel wrapped with Christmas lights. He brought his class with him for an after hours field trip. He sat with his back towards his students, but every once in a while, he turned his head to yell something at them, and then there would be a flashing of lights from their phones. Lune walked over to Stevie, looked over his shoulder and saw that he was making sigils, the ink from his pen flowing on his notebook, little cenotes in the palm of his hand. Carlo was braiding glow tape in the shiny hair of tourist women for ten dollars a head.

Nico sat on the east side of the cenote, lighting skinny sticks at the tips and tossing them into the water. Lune looked at him from across the way. He mouthed the word, *copal*, even though she already knew what he was burning. The chatting of tourists turned to a slow murmur as Marcrina walked out of the pink house wearing her daffodil dress. She noticed that her mother was barefoot as she walked on the earth, under the lights, cool and white and florescent. Lune could feel the tremor of the tree roots as her mother walked over them, and she could feel the itch in between her mother's toes, and the blood red ants at her mother's feet. Lune saw Marcrina sit next to her grandson, and Lune could smell the orange of the copal, the burning of tree sap, the open and shut of Marcrina's eyes, the holes that began to weep in that gash of the earth. Lune saw her mother's tears touch the water, blue green. She saw the tears illuminate the water. Lune saw the slant of her son's eyes and the way he pulled his grandmother's hair away from her face, her throat scream bleeding free into the cenote, paying no mind to the souls floating around, snapping pictures. Her throat wailed and the water from her face gave its offering to her ancestors.

And on that night, the cenote spoke back to her. The water began to seep and rush under her feet. The water began to rush at the four corners of the cenote, the perfect O of it gave its fullest to Marcrina and Nico. Lune saw the cenote water sweep away her mother and her son underneath the long limbed trees like a lullaby. The screams of the tourists began to teeter away from the pink house. The snapping of their phones was like a shutter of lights and heat and mist. Dry heat and trees and cenote water. There was the roar of cars and buses, and the water splash under tires. The overturning of a taco grill, its meat spilled out and skimming across the water, turning to fish. Lune trudged through the water, skin and bones heavy, blood screaming for her flesh and her flesh and her flesh.

# ORBIT/UARY

MARCRINA LOPEZ WAS a mother and a grand-mother. She was one of the organizers that led the revolts against the hospitals. She delivered the dead infants of brown women who could not afford to pay the expense of traveling to the other side of the mountains. Every night, three hundred and sixty-five days a year, visitors made pilgrimages to see her cry into the cenote on the outskirts of the city. There will be a plaque dedicated in her honor at Cenote City Park, where she spent much of her girlhood. She is survived by her daughter, Lune Lopez.

# M ONSTRUA

KNOW that my mother didn't die from the water. My mother died from poison that she took gently into her mouth. Poison swimming like fish that don't belong in a cenote. The same poison that we had pulled from my son's mouth on his birthday. The poison that she put in her apron pocket for safekeeping. If only we could tear these days back like a zipper, make room for the night in our mouths. She wanted the fish to be the color of Nico, burning alive. Nico's body lost in the water spilling over. This was his burial. She chose to die. My mother grew up watching movies at the drive-in where the girl monster always gets killed in the end. My mother died inside her pink house, the wallpaper peeling at the corner, exposing the small bits of drywall like snow, the nails fluttering with her small choking breath like moths in that snow. It hardly ever snows in this city. My mother chose her flower.

# BLACK SAGE

THERE'S a buzz of flies around my mother's pink house, and I can hear Lucy our ghost dog, walking along the wood floor, tapping her claws on the floor like it was the earth. The dirt feels warm and wet under my feet. Warmed by the sun that will brown my skin to the color of my youth, again and again and again. My friends light candles for me at their windows and wait for me. *Come and find me*, I say. There is a canal out there with tangled grocery carts and love letters with calligraphy and a blonde hospital doll, but there is no river here. Jonny comes to my mother's yard to see me. The ducks have come back and walk in circles, their tiny mouths lined with floating teeth like prayers and an altar boy's candles, and I wait at the lip of the cenote pool, blue and embryonic.

*Come with me*, Jonny says.

He wants me to go with him to the other side, where there is no pink house emptied of my mother and my son. Jonny's hands have lost their tremble. They are still and they will climb over the mountains that have rocked this valley, since I was a girl. I'll tell Jonny to go away and he'll leave alone because I asked him to and he listens when I speak. He'll drive away in his tiny hospital truck with clean needles and bandages and all the yellow light bulbs not lost in the deluge. He'll try to hide me away in holes, places dug from dirt, he'll trace the song and put it to his mouth, still unafraid to say my name because he wants to protect his friend.

Tonight, I'll light the sage into smoke, the new color of my son's hair, drum beat, a dream passing in the mouth of the cenote, and I'll wait and I'll wait, and when he calls me to dive, I'll swim in blues and greens in my black dress, a flute in my hand, and I'll find him there where salt water meets fresh water, sitting along the embankment, reading his book, and I'll watch my love make fire under water.

racias

THANK you to my mother for bringing me stories and to my father for helping me to tell mine. Thank you to my brother, Matthew and my sister, Miranda for laughing with me. It's my favorite thing! Thank you to Tino Juarez for your unparalleled love and support. Thank you to my Quintana and Resendez families. Thank you to the Juarez and Otero families.

IMMENSE THANKS to Leza Cantoral and Christoph Paul for supporting my work. Writing this book was a blessing and I'll forever be grateful for CLASH.

THANK you to Joel Amat Güell, Rios de la Luz, Gabino Iglesias, and Sarah Chavez for being generous with your work and your time.

INFINITE THANKS to Jacob Hernandez and Steven Sanchez for seeing me through the writing of this book and so many things. Thank you to Jackie Huertaz and Jonathan Leggett for being angels and empaths. Thank you to Mia Barraza Martinez, Carleigh Takemoto, Kamilah Okafor, and Nicole Tala-mantez for your power and beauty.

THANK you to those that encouraged me in my most difficult year. I won't ever forget it: Monica Limón, Nicole Henares, Brenda Venezia, Kourtnie McKenzie, Fernanda Lemus, Teresa Chacón, Sara Borjas, Rebecca Gonzales, Alma Rosa Rivera, Sylvia Savala, Marissa Raigoza, Carribean Fragoza, Aideed Medina, Marisol Baca, Nancy Hernandez, Jamie Moore, José Angel Araguz, David Campos, Juan Luis Guzmán, Anthony Cody, Mickey Chacón, Romeo Guzman, Sean Kinneen, and Jefferson Beavers.

THANKS TO MY BRAVE TEACHER, Randa Jarrar for showing me I can be a mother and a writer.

THANKS to the Sundress Academy for the Arts for giving me the quiet time and space to write much of this book. Thank you to Lisa Marie Basile and the editors at Luna Luna Magazine. Thank you to the editors at Five 2 One Magazine and Tropics of Meta.

THANK YOU TO MY SON, Isaiah Juarez. Nothing, I mean nothing, means more to me than being you mother. May you manifest things daily.

Monique Quintana was born and raised in the Central Valley, "the other California" and holds an MFA in Creative Writing from CSU Fresno. She is a Senior Associate Editor at Luna Luna Magazine, Fiction Editor at Five-2-One Magazine, and a contributor at CLASH Media. She blogs about Latinx Literature at her site, bloodmoonblog.com, and her work has appeared in Winter Tangerine, Queen Mob's Tea House, Grimoire, Huizache: The Magazine for Latino Literature, and The Acentos Review, among other publications. She is an alumna of the Sundress Academy for the Arts and has been nominated for Best of the Net. She is a Pocha Xicana and still working on herself. You can find her at moniquequintana1@gmail.com

Twitter @quintanagothic IG @quintanadarkling

ALSO BY CLASH BOOKS

**TRAGEDY QUEENS: STORIES INSPIRED BY LANA DEL REY & SYLVIA PLATH**

Edited by Leza Cantoral

**GIRL LIKE A BOMB**

Autumn Christian

**THIS BOOK IS BROUGHT TO YOU BY MY STUDENT LOANS**

Megan J. Kaleita

**DARK MOONS RISING IN A STARLESS NIGHT**

Mame Bougouma Diene

**NOHO GLOAMING & THE CURIOUS CODA OF ANTHONY SANTOS**

Daniel Knauf (Creator of HBO's Carnivàle)

**99 POEMS TO CURE WHATEVER'S WRONG WITH YOU OR CREATE THE PROBLEMS YOU NEED**

Sam Pink

**FOGHORN LEGHORN**

Big Bruiser Dope Boy

## IF YOU DIED TOMORROW I WOULD EAT YOUR CORPSE

Wrath James White

## THE ANARCHIST KOSHER COOKBOOK

Maxwell Bauman

## HORROR FILM POEMS

Christoph Paul

## NIGHTMARES IN ECTASY

Brendan Vidito

## THE VERY INEFFECTIVE HAUNTED HOUSE

Jeff Burk

## ZOMBIE PUNKS FUCK OFF

Edited by Sam Richard

## THIS BOOK AIN'T NUTTIN TO FUCK WITH: A WU-TANG TRIBUTE ANTHOLOGY

Edited by Christoph Paul & Grant Wamack

## WALK HAND IN HAND INTO EXTINCTION - STORIES INSPIRED BY TRUE DETECTIVE

Edited by Christoph Paul & Leza Cantoral